ADVENTURE ISLAND

THE MYSTERY
OF THE CURSED RUBY

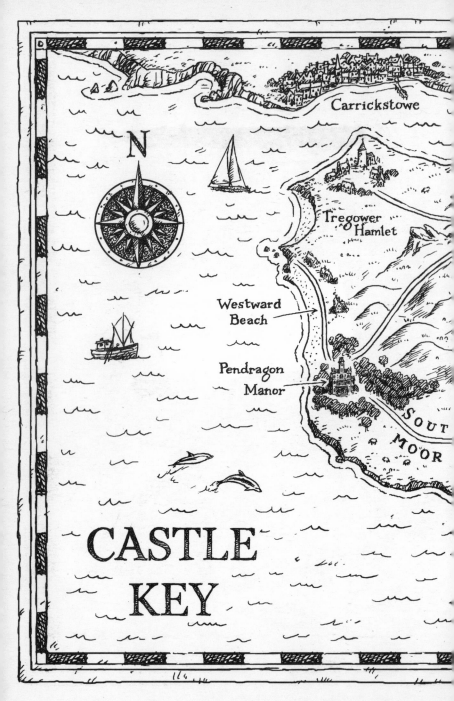

Carrickstowe

N

Tregower
Hamlet

Westward
Beach

Pendragon
Manor

SOUT
MOOR

CASTLE
KEY

Collect all the Adventure Island *books*

ADVENTURE ISLAND

THE MYSTERY OF THE
CURSED
RUBY

Helen Moss

Illustrated by Leo Hartas

Orion
Children's Books

First published in Great Britain in 2011
by Orion Children's Books
a division of the Orion Publishing Group Ltd
Orion House
5 Upper St Martin's Lane
London WC2H 9EA
An Hachette UK company

3 5 7 9 10 8 6 4 2

A catalogue record for this book
is available from the British Library.

ISBN 978 1 4440 0332 1

Printed and bound in Great Britain by
Clays Ltd, St Ives plc

For Mum and Dad

One

The Circus Comes to Town

'The circus starts tonight. We've got to go!'

Emily Wild scrambled up onto the sun-baked rocks and sat hugging her little dog Drift and gazing out over Pirate Cove. The Romaldi Circus always came to Castle Key for the last week of the summer holidays and Emily had gone every year she could remember. This year the theme of the show was the Arabian Nights. She couldn't wait!

But Scott wasn't exactly jumping up and down with excitement. He'd noticed the circus setting up on the common, of course. You could hardly *miss* a convoy of trucks and caravans and a red-and-yellow-striped big top. Especially when it was only a few minutes away from Stone Cottage, where he and Jack were staying for the summer with their Great-aunt Kate. But weren't circuses a bit on the *cheesy* side? Clowns with silly shoes and red noses squirting each other with water? That sounded right up there at the gorgonzola end of the cheesiness scale.

His younger brother Jack was more enthusiastic. 'I'm up for it!' he said, rummaging through the picnic bag for a packet of crisps. 'As long as there's a lion-tamer with *really* ferocious lions. Oh, and some tigers.'

'Jack Carter!' Emily cried, aiming a sandwich crust at his head. 'They don't have animals, apart from a horse and a poodle. Making wild animals perform tricks would be cruel!'

'Yeah, *obviously*! I was joking!' Jack said, back-tracking rapidly. 'What *do* they have then?'

'Oh, acrobats, sword-swallowers, flying trapeze . . . It's *amazing!*'

'Sword-swallowers?' Jack echoed. '*Now* you're talking!' He threw back his head, and did a revoltingly realistic sword-swallowing mime using the last crisp. 'Anyone fancy another swim?'

Drift pricked up his ears, the black one *and* the white

one with brown spots. *Swim* was one of his favourite words!

Scott stretched and pretended he wasn't interested. Then he leaped up and took off across the scorching sand towards the waves. 'Last one in buys the circus tickets!' he shouted over his shoulder.

—

Scott had to admit Emily was right. Sitting in the front row of the packed big top, he couldn't help being seriously impressed by the Romaldi Circus. The show opened with a dramatic laser light display and swirling Arabian music. Suddenly they were plunged into darkness. Stars gradually twinkled into life all over the roof of the big top. Flying carpets began swooping in from every direction and hovering above the circus ring. The performers hopped down from the carpets, backflipping and cartwheeling around the ring in a welcome parade. And that was just the opening sequence.

Sitting between Scott and Jack, with Drift curled up on her lap, Emily joined in the applause. But beneath the excitement, she couldn't help feeling a trace of sadness. Coming to the circus meant the summer holidays were almost over. And what a summer it had been – full of secret passages, flooded caves, ghosts, film stars, buried treasure and stolen masterpieces. But soon Scott and Jack's dad would be back from his archaeological dig in Africa. The boys would be going home to London. School loomed just over the horizon. Emily didn't *mind* school in principle but it took up valuable time she'd much rather spend conducting important investigations.

Emily jumped as Jack nudged her arm and shook a bag of popcorn under her nose. She snapped back to reality and settled down to enjoy the show. The ringmaster was galloping around on a magnificent white horse. Enzo Romaldi – a stern-looking old man with bushy white eyebrows and moustache – was dressed as a sultan in a fabulous jewelled turban and cloak. He pulled the horse up in the middle of the ring and introduced the first act. '. . . the Sword of Persia, a man who laughs in the face of peril . . .'

Jack craned forward in his seat. 'Sounds like my kind of guy!'

Accompanied by the beating of gongs, a huge copper-coloured man burst into the ring, juggling six mighty scimitars, their blades flashing in the spotlights. He was wearing leggings and wrist-guards of tooled leather and a metal breastplate. His back was tattooed with crossed swords. To Jack's delight, the Sword of Persia wasn't content with just *swallowing* swords; he set them alight and *then* swallowed three of them, while hanging upside-down over a bed of nails.

'Don't try this at home!' Emily whispered to Jack.

'Spoilsport!' Jack brandished his stick of candy-floss like a flaming sword.

Scott shook his head. 'I'm telling Aunt Kate to lock the cutlery drawer!'

For his next trick, the Sword inserted six long swords into a giant Ali Baba jar. He tipped the jar over to show the audience how the blades criss-crossed inside. Then he removed the swords and his assistant – a lady in a belly-dancing outfit – climbed inside. She smiled and waved as the Sword of Persia placed the lid on the jar. Slowly, he slid the swords into the jar again, jiggling each one a little until the tip poked out through a small hole on the other side.

Emily cringed. She could almost *feel* the cold metal blades on her skin. Of course, she knew the lady wasn't *really* being stabbed. There had to be a trick to that jar. She wished she could get inside and see how it worked. At last, the Sword of Persia drew the swords out and sliced the air with a flourish and a cry of *Open Sesame!* The assistant jumped out and belly-danced around the ring – not a puncture wound in sight.

'How did they do that?' Jack marvelled. 'I thought she'd be skewered like a kebab.'

'False bottom!' Scott said knowledgeably.

'I dunno. It looks real to me!' Jack laughed, glancing at the belly-dancer's wiggling hips.

The Sword of Persia was followed by acrobats and jugglers and a contortionist who folded herself up inside tiny boxes and bags. There was an incredible mind-reading act called Incognito. He was a sinister figure, in lizard-green body paint and a long black cloak, who appeared like a genie from a giant golden lamp in Aladdin's cave, and could somehow guess people's secret wishes. Then Mimi the poodle took to the ring. Her trainer played the part of the bored Princess Jasmine, locked in a tower. Mimi – her fur dyed pale pink and sporting a veil and jewelled headband – pulled off amazing balancing tricks to fetch beautiful objects to amuse the princess.

'I thought *you* were the smartest dog in town, Drift,' Scott joked, 'but I bet you couldn't do that.'

'He could if he *wanted* to!' Emily said loyally. 'But how often is he going to need to walk backwards along a tightrope?'

Drift's ears pricked up as he watched. But whether he was more interested in Mimi's sensational sense of balance or her cute little pom-pom tail, it was hard to tell.

The grand finale was the trapeze act. The Flying Romaldis' breathtaking display told a story of young princesses who turned into birds to escape from their palace, and were then pursued by evil guards. Emily watched in amazement as a girl – not much older than she was – swan-dived from the very pinnacle of the big top. Just as it seemed she would free-fall into the audience, one of the men caught her and tossed her back up into the air to land on a tiny platform.

'Wow!' Scott said. 'These guys are good!'

'Good?' Jack laughed. 'They're awesome!' Spellbound, he watched as the girl swooped overhead again. She let go of the swing, caught it with her feet, then sprang backwards; one flip, two flips and here was the guy flying in to catch her again as she soared past. She reached for his outstretched arms but at the last moment he seemed to draw back. The girl lunged for his wrists again and then grabbed at an empty trapeze. But it was too late.

The entire audience gasped.

Then there was a terrible silence as the girl spun out over the edge of the safety net and plummeted to the ground.

Two

Quick Thinking and Decisive Action

The sound of the girl's body hitting the ground made Jack's stomach turn over. She'd landed in the aisle just a few metres away. She looked as tiny and fragile as a hummingbird, with a strand of her long dark hair across her face and her left leg bent at an angle that just wasn't meant for legs.

A crowd instantly gathered around the motionless figure, but everyone stood aside as a tall man in a sparkly crimson costume pushed through and sank to his knees. 'Gina!' he cried, holding out his arms to scoop the girl up.

'Noooo!' Jack yelled. 'Don't do that!' They'd done life-saving training at school and although Jack wasn't exactly known for being the best listener on the planet – there were hyperactive goldfish with longer attention spans – he remembered one thing: *if someone falls onto their back you shouldn't move them.* He sprang out of his seat and rugby-tackled the Flying Romaldi guy to the ground.

'Get off!' The man lashed out trying to dislodge Jack from his back. He was big and strong, with biceps the size of basketballs.

Well, if you're going to pick fights with trapeze artists, Jack told himself, *you've got to expect that upper body strength comes as standard!* He was wondering how much longer he could cling on, when an elderly woman stepped out of the crowd, shooing people away. 'I'm a doctor!' she announced in a commanding voice.

The Flying Romaldi shook Jack off with a mighty jerk of his shoulders, then dropped his head in his hands and stepped back. The doctor felt the girl's neck for a pulse and looked under her eyelids. 'Unconscious but breathing. Someone call an ambulance!'

Scott held up his phone. 'I'm on it.'

'Jolly good!' the doctor barked. She turned to face the Flying Romaldi guy. 'Is this your daughter?'

'Yes,' the man sobbed. 'Gina!' He reached out to hold her again.

The doctor pushed his hands away. 'No! You *never* move a patient if there's any chance of a spinal injury. Wait for the paramedics.'

'Oh, OK, sorry,' the man mumbled, letting his arms drop to his sides. 'I panicked.'

'Of course,' the doctor said, a little more gently. 'Now, *this* young man had the right idea!' She beamed at Jack. 'Well done. Your quick thinking and decisive action may well have saved this unfortunate girl from being paralyzed!'

Jack grinned. *Quick thinking and decisive action!* He liked the sound of that!

—

Next morning Jack and Scott were in the kitchen at Stone Cottage polishing off a cooked breakfast. Jack was telling Aunt Kate, *yet again*, how he'd leaped to the rescue at the circus. Scott sighed. He was proud of what Jack had done, of course, but if he heard the words *quick thinking and decisive action* one more time, he was going to have to lock his brother in the shed at the bottom of the garden and throw away the key.

Jack's story was interrupted by the doorbell. Aunt Kate returned to the kitchen with a dark-haired man, so tall he had to duck to avoid head-butting the low wooden beams. Scott did a double take before recognizing him as the trapeze girl's father; his outfit of jeans and white polo shirt was a long way from yesterday's sequined leotard arrangement.

The man grasped Jack's hand. 'I'm Luca Romaldi. I wanted to thank you for what you did yesterday.'

'How *is* your daughter now?' Aunt Kate asked, handing him a mug of coffee.

Luca took a sip. 'Gina has a broken leg and some bruising. They're keeping her in Carrickstowe Hospital for a few days. But it could have been much worse, if it hadn't been for our hero here!'

Aunt Kate smiled and peered over her glasses at Jack. 'So I've been hearing.'

Jack grinned. 'Cheers! It was nothing!' He was *trying* to act like a modest and humble hero instead of the annoying big-headed kind. But he couldn't help feeling pleased with himself. Scott 'Teenage Hero' Carter had been hogging the limelight for daredevil rescue bids since saving that Hartley kid in The House Of Horrors during Operation Gold.

'Gina would like to thank you in person,' Luca Romaldi was saying. 'I'm going to the hospital now if you'd like to come? And Scott too, of course,' he added. 'I heard you called the ambulance. Thank you.'

Scott smiled. Calling nine, nine, nine was hardly a major deal. But it was nice of Luca to share out some of Jack's glory. 'Can our friend, Emily, come too?' he asked.

'Of course,' Luca said. 'We'll pick her up on the way.'

Gina's younger sister, Bella, was sitting in the front of the car but she spent the whole journey, across Castle Key island and over the causeway to the mainland, twisting round in her seat to chat to the three friends in the back. She was twelve – the same age as Jack and Emily – small and slim with dark sparkling eyes and black hair in a single plait that reached almost to her waist.

Emily soon realized that being an amazing trapeze artist wasn't Bella Romaldi's only major talent; she could also talk at dizzying speed without coming up for air. Normally, when Emily met someone new, she had to ask lots of questions to build up a complete profile – you never knew when such background information could come in useful for later investigations – but with Bella, there was no need.

'You three are so lucky. I don't really have any friends my own age,' Bella said, 'because we're always travelling around. I've got my sister, Gina, of course. She's two years older than me and she's cool, but I wish I could go to a proper school with classrooms and teachers and all that . . .'

'Whoah!' Jack threw his hands up to hold back the tide of Bella's chatter. 'Let's just rewind that bit. You live in a circus. You get to do a flying trapeze act every day. Your life is totally awesome. *And you wish you could go to school? Are you insane?*'

Bella laughed. 'We still have to do school work. We train all morning and then we have shows in the evening. We have lessons at home in the afternoon. My Mum's a real slave-driver.'

Jack was starting to see Bella's point. The only good thing about school as far as he was concerned was mucking about with his mates. All the work but with no friends would really suck!

⁓

Gina was propped up on pillows with her leg in a plaster cast, but she smiled as her visitors arrived. Luca went off to fetch a drink for her, while Bella, Emily, Scott and Jack pulled up chairs round the bed.

Jack lapped up Gina's heartfelt thanks for his help. 'Oh yeah, nothing to it!' he said, sticking his hands in his pockets and swaggering around the bed – as if rescuing damsels in distress was all in a day's work.

Scott rolled his eyes.

Emily let Jack enjoy his moment of glory. Then she got down to business. 'Gina, do you have any idea what caused you to fall?'

Scott couldn't believe it. You were supposed to ask people in hospital how they were feeling or whether they'd like a grape, not start interrogating them about their accident! But Emily just couldn't resist trying to get to the bottom of things – preferably *dark, suspicious, criminal* things. In Emily World the ropes had, no doubt, been sabotaged by a ruthless gang of rival trapeze artists. She'd be whipping out her notebook and taking a statement next.

But to Scott's surprise, Gina was happy to talk about it.

'I've been going over and over it in my mind,' she said. 'We've done that catch a thousand times. Danny's never fluffed it before.'

'Who's Danny?' Jack asked.

'He's our creep of a cousin. *His* Dad, Uncle Tony, is *our* Dad's older brother,' Bella explained. 'Danny thinks he's the boss of us just because he's sixteen and because he's a *boy*. No offence!' She grinned at Scott and Jack. 'I wouldn't be surprised if he missed Gina on purpose.'

Gina's mouth dropped open. 'Bella! Don't be silly. Even Danny wouldn't do something like that! Anyway it was my own stupid fault I missed the safety net.'

'What do you mean?' Scott asked.

'Well, we're trained to fall safely if something goes wrong. But I was so desperate not to mess up the catch that I tried to grab another swing and ended up catapulting myself right over the edge of the net.'

Back from the vending machine, Luca Romaldi handed Gina a bottle of sparkling water. 'I'm going to extend that safety net to make sure it can never happen again.'

Gina took the bottle. 'So, have you decided?'

Luca nodded seriously. 'Yes, Bella can take your part tonight.'

Bella leaped into her Dad's arms. 'Thank you! I can't wait!' Then she turned to her new friends. 'They only usually let me do the baby stuff, because I'm the youngest, but I'm perfectly capable of doing all Gina's big moves; I do them in training all the time.'

Luca smiled and turned to Scott, Emily and Jack. 'How would you like to come along and see Bella in action? It's Saturday, so there's a matinee show this afternoon. In fact, we'd better get going because this young lady needs to run through that swan-dive a few more times!'

Bella made a face at her Dad. Then she did a cartwheel and a backflip back to Gina's side. 'See you tomorrow.'

'Good luck,' Gina said. Then she laughed and tapped her plaster cast. 'Break a leg! Isn't that what they say in the theatre?'

Three

Another Near-Disaster

The circus was just as good the second time around. But shortly before the Flying Romaldis came on, disaster almost struck again. Two clowns were chasing each other around in a hilarious fight scene, playing the parts of rival merchants in an Eastern bazaar. They ran up and down poles and tight ropes and ladders, using random objects from the market stalls – rolled up carpets, brooms and baskets – to attack each other. It was very fast and very funny.

The accident happened when one of the duo was shimmying to the top of a long swaying pole which was being held in the teeth of the other clown – a giant of a man with gleaming black skin – who was standing on his head halfway up a ladder. Suddenly the pole snapped in two. Somehow the clown at the top – a very short woman – pulled off a death-defying leap and swung to safety on a dangling rope, while the big guy grabbed the two halves of the pole, bashed them together and threw them at his partner like javelins. They both carried on with the tumbling and acrobatics as if it had all been part of the act. But Emily knew that it wasn't.

'That pole didn't break last night,' she whispered.

'I know,' Scott agreed. 'And both the clowns looked really panicky for a second.'

Jack shrugged. 'Are you sure? I thought it was the funniest part.'

'Detailed observation has never been your strong point,' Emily laughed.

At last it was time for Bella's first performance as the star of the trapeze act. Emily crossed her fingers so tightly she gave herself cramp, and could hardly bear to look when Bella launched herself off the high platform in the swan-dive. The near-disaster in the clowns' act had made her even more nervous. What if something went wrong again? But she needn't have worried. The routine went off without a hitch. Bella was superb.

After the show, the friends hurried to the side entrance

of the big top where Bella had arranged to meet them. She'd pulled a tracksuit on over her leotard, her plait was still wound into a tight bun on top of her head and there were traces of glitter on her cheeks.

'You were fantastic!' Emily cried, giving her new friend a hug.

'Awesome!' Jack and Scott agreed, joining in with high-fives.

Hopping from foot to foot, Bella gave them a blow-by-blow account of the whole act. 'I told Danny before we started that if he dropped *me,* I'd flatten him. You should have seen his face! He looked like he'd swallowed a hornet! Come, on I'll show you round . . .'

Bella provided a running commentary as they toured the big top, including the wings – screened-off areas at the sides of the ring where the performers waited between the acts. Then they visited Moonlight, the white stallion, and fed him handfuls of long grass. 'He belongs to my grandfather, Enzo,' Bella explained. 'Grandfather is nice but he's really strict. He has a soft spot for Moonlight, though!'

Finally they came to the caravans where the circus families lived, neatly parked by a stand of chestnut trees. There was a mixture of styles ranging from small, old-fashioned camper vans to enormous, sleek silver trailers. Many of the performers were sitting outside, relaxing after the show.

In front of one of the caravans, a pale wiry man with

jutting cheekbones was entertaining a group of local children who'd stopped to nose around the circus on their way across the common.

'That's Mike Turnbull,' Bella told the others. 'He's Incognito, the mind-reading act.'

Without his green body paint and black cloak and wig, Mike Turnbull looked more like an accountant or a history teacher than an evil genie, Jack thought. He did have freaky eyes though; one was green and the other was almost black.

'Hey, Mr Mind-reader,' a spiky-haired, chubby boy shouted cheekily. 'Bet you can't tell me what I'm thinking right now!'

Mike Turnbull looked up from his cup of tea and regarded the little gang with a mysterious smile. 'The forces of the mind are too powerful to toy with.'

The chubby boy grinned at the girl standing behind him. 'Told you, he's a fake.'

'But you seem to have something in your ear!' Mike touched the side of the boy's head and pulled out a fancy diver's watch.

'Hey, that's mine!' The boy looked down at his bare wrist and then at his friends. 'This guy nicked my watch!'

'Oh, and this must be yours.' Mike held out an earring in the shape of a little dolphin. The girl snatched it out of his hand and ran away.

Jack laughed. 'Hey, that's cool. I love those tricks. I'm going to ask how he does it.'

But before Jack could strike up a conversation with Mike Turnbull, Drift scampered off to say hello to Mimi the poodle, and the friends followed. Mimi was standing on a small table while her owner brushed her fur. She returned Drift's tail-wagging greeting with a token sniff and a cool look. Bella introduced the friends to Mimi's owner, Madame Zelda. Without the Princess Jasmine costume, Madame Zelda was a stout middle-aged lady. Her hair – the same shade of pink as Mimi's fur – was in curlers under a silk scarf.

'My own blend of essential oils,' Madame Zelda explained, tipping liquid out of a small bottle and massaging it into Mimi's coat with fingers as soft and white as marshmallows. 'It gives that glossy shine! Mimi just couldn't *survive* without it, could you, my little schmootly-wootly-pie?'

Schmootly-wootly-pie? Jack avoided catching Scott's eye and gulped back a laugh. Never mind lion-taming. Surely calling your dog *schmootly-wootly-pie* in public was cruelty to animals?

Drift backed away in case Madame Zelda got any ideas. His coat was quite glossy enough with a quick lick and a roll in the dust!

Madame Zelda's canine beauty tips were interrupted by a disturbance in the next caravan. *Crash! Smash!* It sounded as if someone who was a total stranger to hand-eye co-ordination was practicing a plate-spinning routine.

Madame Zelda smiled. 'That'll be Ray and Barbara off again!'

'The fighting market traders,' Bella explained.

'You mean the clowns?' Jack asked.

'*Comedic acrobats*,' Madame Zelda corrected. 'Don't let them hear you call them *clowns*!'

Bella giggled. 'All the fighting isn't only for their act. They're just the same in real life!'

'They've been happily married for twenty years,' Madame Zelda said, shaking her head as the insults kept flying out of the window.

'I thought you checked the equipment this morning, you lazy oaf!' Barbara was yelling.

'F.Y.I. I did check it!' Ray shouted. 'And why do I have to do everything, anyway? You can't even climb up a pole without breaking it. I could get a trained budgie to do it better!'

'All *you* have to do is hold the pole!' Barbara shot back. 'Not exactly rocket science is it? Holding a big stick in your mouth. A Labrador could do it!'

The friends said goodbye to Madame Zelda and Mimi and walked to the last – and biggest – caravan in the row. 'Home, sweet, home,' Bella said, inviting them in.

'Cool!' Scott breathed, as they stepped inside. And he wasn't just talking about the air-conditioning. The caravan was kitted out with high-tech appliances, including an enormous wide-screen TV and a state-of-the-art computer.

Bella's mum was in the kitchen. She was also a member of the Flying Romaldis but had changed out of her leotard into jeans and t-shirt. To Jack's astonishment she ambushed him with an enormous hug. 'Thank you for helping Gina yesterday,' she said. 'I'm Sylvia.'

Jack backed away, grinning. 'Oh *that*, it was just . . .'

'. . . *quick thinking and decisive action!*' Scott, Emily and Bella chorused. It was becoming something of a catchphrase.

'Well, *whatever* it was, we're grateful!' Sylvia hugged Scott and Emily for good measure. 'Make yourselves at home,' she said, popping open a big cake tin. 'Now, I hope you like chocolate cake?'

Jack stared at her. Was there the remotest possibility that there was someone on the planet who *didn't* like chocolate cake? He inhaled the fresh-baked aroma that was wafting from the tin.

'It's got caramel fudge icing,' Sylvia said.

'Yeah, I think I can probably force it down.' Jack helped himself to the largest piece on the plate. *This is the life*, he thought, flopping down on a sofa and putting his feet up. Well, he *had* been told to make himself at home. It'd be rude not to. Computer, telly *and* chocolate cake. All of life's essentials within easy reach. *Maybe I will run away with the circus after all!*

'I'm just going over to see Ray and Barbara,' Sylvia called from the kitchen. 'I'll take them some chocolate cake to cheer them up.'

'Usually works for me!' Jack said, helping himself to another piece.

As the door shut behind her mum, Bella suddenly looked serious and shook her head. 'It's so weird, two accidents happening in a row. First Gina's fall and then that pole snapping like that. It's almost as if the ruby has lost its powers or something . . .'

Four

The Eye of Fire

'Run that past me again, Bella,' Scott said through a mouthful of caramel fudge icing. 'It *almost* sounded as if you said *the ruby has lost its powers!*'

Bella blushed. 'Oh, er, did I? Well it's just one of those family things, you know?'

'Um, not really,' Jack laughed. 'Last time I checked, we didn't have any jewels with magic powers in *our* family. How about you, Em? Got any enchanted emeralds tucked away at The Lighthouse?'

Emily grinned and shook her head. 'What *did* you mean about the ruby, Bella?'

Bella sat down next to her and hugged one of the sofa cushions to her chest. 'I shouldn't have said anything. We're not meant to tell outsiders about it.'

Scott raised his eyebrows at Jack and Emily. Not only was there a ruby with powers, it was a *secret* ruby with powers. One thing was certain: there was no way someone as nosy as Emily was going to leave the caravan until she had the full story, even if she had to stay there all night. 'We don't want you to tell us if you're not allowed to, Bella,' Scott said kindly, even though he was bursting to find out about this magical ruby too.

'Speak for yourself! *I* do!' Jack spluttered. 'Come on, Bella, spill!'

'We won't tell a soul,' Emily coaxed. 'And you can't leave us in suspense now. That'd be mental cruelty.'

Bella laughed. 'Well, actually, I think it *would* be OK if I told you guys. After all, you're not really outsiders any more.' She tucked her legs underneath her on the sofa and got comfortable. 'The ruby is called the Eye of Fire and it was given to my great, great, great, great grandfather, Francesco Romaldi, by an Indian maharajah . . .'

'Cool,' Jack said. 'I'm loving this story already.'

'The Romaldi family were world-famous trapeze

artists even back then,' Bella continued. 'They were in India putting on a special show for this maharajah and his family, when the palace was besieged by the army of a neighbouring state. The soldiers were killing everyone and . . .'

'Marauding? Pillaging?' Jack suggested.

'Yeah, there was a lot of marauding and pillaging,' Bella agreed. 'Anyway, the soldiers were streaming into the palace, cutting off the servants' heads with these huge, flashing swords and stuffing all the treasures into coffers and loading them onto their elephants. The maharajah and his family had to flee for their lives, but before they left, the maharajah ran into the palace temple and prised out this massive ruby from the statue of Ganesha . . .'

'Ganesha?' Emily asked. 'Is that the Hindu god with the elephant's head?'

'Yes, that's right. The ruby was the mystical third eye of the statue, set into the middle of its forehead. Even as the soldiers were smashing down the doors of the temple, the maharajah thrust the ruby into Francesco Romaldi's hands and asked him to smuggle it out of the palace so it wouldn't fall into the possession of his enemies.

'"Ganesha's sacred ruby can never be truly owned by anyone," the maharajah explained. "It was entrusted to my family for safe-keeping many centuries ago. Now I pass the guardianship of the Eye of Fire to the Romaldi family. It will keep you safe and bring you good fortune. But it must never leave your family until it is recalled by the gods . . ."' Bella paused for breath.

'Wow! Then what happened?' Jack was so enthralled he forgot to chew his cake.

Bella continued the story. She'd clearly heard the tale many times and knew it by heart. 'At that moment they heard the terrible sound of the temple doors crashing to the ground. The palace guards held the hordes back long enough for some of the family to get out through a secret door, but the maharajah and his wife were killed. The Romaldis escaped from the temple by leaping from the windows and swinging down on the vines that clung to the walls. But in his hurry,' Bella went on, 'Francesco dropped the ruby. It would have been lost, except that it was caught by his youngest granddaughter, Leonora, as it fell to the ground. The ruby has been in the care of the Romaldi family since that day. True to the maharajah's word, it has kept us safe and brought us good fortune.'

'That's an amazing story,' Scott said. 'It's like something from the Arabian Nights.' *But surely that's all it is,* he thought. *A story.* 'You don't *really* believe that this ruby has the power to protect your family, do you?'

Bella looked puzzled – as if he'd asked if she *really* believed that electricity had the power to make the lights come on. 'Of course! That's why the Flying Romaldis can do such dangerous moves that no other groups dare to perform. The ruby looks after us.'

'But then Gina had her accident,' Emily said. 'And that pole broke today. *That's* what you meant when you said the ruby had lost its powers.'

'Oh, I didn't *mean* it!' Bella said hurriedly.

But Emily's suspicions were already running away with her. The legend said that the ruby would protect the Romaldis as long they kept it safe. 'What if someone has *stolen* the ruby?' she asked. 'That would explain why it's not protecting you any more?'

Bella smiled and shook her head. 'Oh, no, that's impossible!'

'Nothing's *impossible*!' Jack laughed. 'Well, except for quadratic equations maybe.'

'There's no way anyone could take the ruby,' Bella said. 'It's kept in a casket built into grandfather's caravan. Francesco Romaldi had it specially made from the hardest ebony to house the ruby. And it's got this special locking mechanism made by the finest clockmakers in Switzerland. There are three separate keys and they all have to be turned in the locks at the same time. And the keys belong to three different members of the family.'

'Who are the key-holders?' Emily asked.

'One key's always kept by the head of the family, of course. That's my grandfather. Then it's usually his oldest son. That's Uncle Tony. But they had a big row a few weeks ago and Grandfather took his key off him and gave it to my dad, even though he's younger.'

'Good on him!' Jack laughed, sticking his tongue out

at Scott. 'Why should *eldest* brothers get all the breaks anyway?'

'And who's the third key-holder?' Emily asked.

'Well,' Bella said smiling, 'remember how it was the youngest granddaughter who saved the ruby in the escape from the temple? Because of that, it's always the youngest girl in the family who has the third key.' She held up her arm. A delicate silver charm bracelet jangled on her wrist. 'Ta da! It's me!'

The friends examined the slender silver key hanging on the bracelet. It was beautiful, with an intricate flower pattern worked at one end, and tiny teeth at the other.

'Sounds like this ruby's got more security than the Crown Jewels,' Jack laughed.

'It has,' Bella replied seriously. 'We check on it every single morning at dawn. The whole family gathers in Grandfather's caravan before we start our day's training. We open the casket so we can pay our respects to the ruby and ask for its protection for the coming day. Then we lock it all up again. There's absolutely no way anyone could steal the Eye of Fire.' Suddenly Bella's hand shot to her mouth. 'Oh, dear! I really shouldn't have told you all that. Grandfather would be furious if he found out. I'm always getting into trouble for talking too much.'

Emily smiled. 'Don't worry. Your secret is safe with us.'

'Yeah,' Jack said. 'We've forgotten every word already.'

'Ruby? What, ruby?' Scott asked.

Bella looked relieved. 'Thanks, guys. I knew I could trust you.'

—

That night Emily was so excited she could barely sleep. She pictured the keys turning in the locks, the lid of the casket creaking open, a sumptuous red velvet cushion, and on that cushion . . . *nothing*! The more Bella had insisted the ruby *couldn't* be stolen, the more convinced Emily was that someone *had* swiped it. She was so sure, in fact, that she was already planning the investigation to find the thief. She'd even written a new heading in her notebook – *OPERATION RUBY* – and underlined it twice.

Emily checked her alarm clock for the hundredth time. She'd set it for quarter to five in the morning, because when the Romaldi family gathered at dawn, Emily planned to be peeping in through the little window at the back of Enzo's caravan – the one that she had just happened to notice as they were saying goodbye to Bella. She was going to witness the empty casket with her own eyes. She couldn't wait!

Operation Ruby could be their most exciting case yet!

Five

A Whole New Adventure

When Emily and the boys arranged to meet at the circus in the morning to watch the Romaldi family open the ruby casket, Jack had naturally assumed she meant about ten-thirty – just before elevenses, perhaps. It was only *after* Jack and Scott had agreed to the plan, that the D-word was mentioned.

'Weren't you listening to Bella?' Emily had asked, rolling her eyes. 'The Romaldis ask the Eye of Fire for its blessing *at dawn*. Then they do rehearsals and fitness work for the rest of the morning.'

Which is why Jack found himself crouched behind Enzo Romaldi's caravan stupidly early in the morning. Emily and Drift were there, looking bright and alert, as if they leaped out of bed to watch the sunrise every morning. Scott, on the other hand, looked as lively as a zombie with a migraine. Cautiously, they peeped through the window. The Romaldis were all squeezed into the living room of the caravan. Bella was perched on the arm of a sofa, next to her parents. Emily also recognized the other two members of the Flying Romaldis – Bella's Uncle Tony and her cousin Danny, a scowling boy with the broad, muscle-bound shoulders of a pit bull terrier. The slim blonde woman sitting next to Uncle Tony must be his wife, Anna, Emily guessed, also known as Anna-lastica, the contortionist act.

Ray and Barbara, the comedic acrobats, were there too and so was Madame Zelda, with Mimi on her lap. Bella had explained that Barbara and Zelda were also members of the extended Romaldi family – third cousins twice removed, or something. Everyone wore tracksuits ready for their training session – except for Madame Zelda and Mimi, who were modelling matching pink silk dressing gowns.

Bella's grandfather, Enzo Romaldi, stood up and raised one finger. Although elderly, he was still a powerfully built man. Beneath his charming smile, he exuded the confidence of someone who was used to being in charge.

The chatter in the room stopped instantly. Enzo walked to the back wall and pulled a string to open a thick tasselled curtain. An antique desk was revealed. The polished wood was so dark it was almost black and it had hundreds of tiny compartments and drawers, each with miniature golden handles. On top of the desk was a casket the size of a large shoebox, carved with dancing elephants and decorated with gold leaf.

Enzo beckoned for Bella and her dad to join him. Then he held up a small silver key attached to a chain around his neck. Luca flipped open the back of his watch and took out a matching silver key. Bella slipped her charm bracelet from her wrist. Solemnly, they inserted their keys into keyholes concealed in the carvings around the edge of the casket.

Emily held her breath as the three keys were turned in unison. Enzo placed both hands on the casket and slowly lifted the lid.

'Wow!' Jack breathed.

'Cool!' Scott murmured.

'*What?*' Emily spluttered.

Emily couldn't believe it. The ruby definitely *hadn't* been stolen, because it was sitting there, glowing in the morning sunlight, and casting glittering red reflections onto its pillow of white satin, like fire on water.

Scott whistled. 'That thing's the size of a cricket ball!'

'It's some serious bling,' Jack agreed.

But Emily couldn't help feeling disappointed. True, the ruby was fabulous. But why hadn't someone *stolen* it? She was going to have to cross out *OPERATION RUBY* in her notebook.

Now Enzo was addressing the ruby in a low voice. The friends could only catch a few words: *Eye of Fire . . . request your protection for the coming day . . .* Then the lid was closed and the casket was locked once more. The ritual was over. But suddenly there was an outburst of raised voices inside the caravan.

'Why do we keep up this ridiculous charade?' Uncle Tony shouted, springing out of his chair. 'That ruby's not looking after us any more!' He was broad and solid, like his son Danny but in a larger size and when he banged his fist against the wall the whole caravan shook. 'Wake up and smell the coffee! We've had two major accidents in the last two days. Any "protective powers" it might have had are long gone!'

Luca leaped up and stood nose to nose with his brother. 'Rubbish! Those accidents would have been much worse if the Eye of Fire hadn't protected us.'

Barbara stood up to Tony too, although she only came up to his waist. 'Luca's right. If that rope hadn't been there when the pole snapped I'd have been a goner.'

'And,' Luca went on, 'the ruby sent that young lad, Jack Carter, to watch over Gina when she fell. You're not telling me it was a coincidence that her guardian angel was sitting two seats away?'

The other members of the family murmured their agreement.

Scott felt Jack nudge his elbow.

'Guardian angel!' Jack whispered. 'That's me. I was sent by the Eye of Fire. Special Delivery.'

Scott kicked him. It was way too early in the morning for Jack's bragging.

'Shh!' Emily hissed.

Tony was ranting again. 'If you lot had half a brain cell, you'd see that we're slogging our guts out playing these one-horse dumps, for the few hundred people we can pack into our pathetic little big top.'

'Yeah,' Danny sneered. '*Big* top? It should be called, like, the . . . er, *really small* top.'

Jack snorted. '*Really small top?* Danny Boy's not exactly the master of the witty one-liner, is he?'

'If we sold the ruby we could buy the land we need to open a theme park in Florida or Texas,' Tony went on. 'That's how it could *really* protect us!'

'*Sell the ruby?*' Madame Zelda gasped. 'But you know it can't leave the family.'

Suddenly Enzo spoke and everyone fell silent. 'Tony Romaldi!' he said. 'I'm ashamed to hear my own son speaking like this! I know that you no longer wish to follow our traditions and travel with the circus after this season, which is why I've named Luca as my heir and given him your key to the casket. But to suggest that we *sell* the Eye of Fire is stepping too far over the line. The ruby is not ours to do with as we wish. The maharajah entrusted our family to safeguard the ruby on behalf of the Temple of Ganesha!'

Tony stormed out, slamming the door behind him. Danny yanked the door open and marched out after his father, giving the door an even mightier slam. Anna followed her husband and son out, although she made a point of pulling the door shut gently behind her.

'There's nothing like a nice family get-together,' Scott sighed, as the friends crept away from the window.

'Poor Bella!' Emily said. 'She looked close to tears.'

They sat down in the long grass behind the chestnut trees. The sunshine had already dried the dew. It promised to be another scorching hot day. 'Well, what are we going to do now?' Scott asked.

Emily thought for a moment. She'd been planning to spend the day tracking down an intrepid jewel thief. But since nobody had had the gumption to actually *steal* the ruby, that wasn't going to happen. 'We could go swimming at Polhallow Lake,' she suggested.

That was the best idea Jack had heard all morning. 'And we could take a picnic!'

Drift sat up and panted happily. Along with *swimming*, *picnic* was another of his favourite words. But then he heard something else. He flicked his ears up, sniffed the breeze and caught the scent of human panic.

Now everyone could hear it. 'My baby! Someone's stolen my baby!' The voice was shrill with distress.

Emily's heart skipped a beat. Operation Baby? It didn't quite have the same ring as Operation Ruby, but could this be the start of a whole new adventure!

Six

Operation Poodle

Scott, Jack, Emily and Drift ran back to the circus to find Madame Zelda flapping around in front of her caravan like an oversized hen, her plump elbows pumping and her floral dressing gown billowing around her legs.

'What's happening?' Bella cried, running from the big top to join them.

'Mimi's gone! My poor baby!' Madame Zelda squawked.

'She doesn't even have her sun screen or her mineral water. She'll be *dehydrating*!'

Scott grasped a quivering arm and helped Madame Zelda into a deck chair. 'Jack will get you a glass of water.'

Jack sighed and went inside to fetch the water. If Scott wanted to suck up to hysterical ladies why couldn't he do his own legwork?

'When exactly did you last see Mimi?' Bella asked.

Madame Zelda dabbed at her pillowy bosom with a lace handkerchief. 'We came back from the meeting in Enzo's trailer. Mimi was terribly upset by all the hullaballoo so I told her to have a little sit-down on her daybed to calm her nerves.' Zelda pointed to a velvet dog basket in the shape of a small throne. 'I went inside to make her some of the special tea she likes. But when I came back out,' Madame Zelda gulped back tears, 'she was *gone*.'

Soon everyone was running around looking for Mimi. In the chaos, nobody seemed surprised to find Emily, Scott and Jack at the circus so early in the morning. Bella's mum called the police to report Mimi missing and her dad and grandfather formed a search party.

Mike Turnbull – alias Incognito – offered to check Moonlight's stable, in case Mimi had got shut in there.

'Shouldn't he be able to locate Mimi using his psychic powers or something?' Scott joked.

'I'll search the storage trucks for you,' a rugged-looking

man with flowing dark hair called out in a distinct Irish accent.

'Who was that?' Scott asked.

'Aidan McDonald,' Bella answered. 'He does the act with the knives.'

'Ah yes, the Sword of Persia!' Jack swashbuckled with an imaginary sword. 'What a dude! But I thought he'd be more . . . well, *Persian*.'

Bella smiled. 'The Arabian Nights thing is just for this season. Last year we had a Japanese theme and he was the Samurai Warrior. Before that, the Celtic Blade.'

Madame Zelda threw back her head and stretched out her arms like an opera singer. 'Mimi! Mimi!' she wailed. If there'd been a crystal glass nearby it probably would have shattered.

'Perhaps she just went behind the trees for a widdle?' Jack suggested.

'Mimi doesn't *widdle* behind trees,' Madame Zelda howled. 'She has her own private toilet facilities!' Tears slid down her fleshy cheeks.

'Don't worry,' Emily said, taking Madame Zelda's hand. 'Drift will help to find Mimi. Do you have something that belongs to her so he can pick up her scent?'

Madame Zelda disappeared inside her caravan and came out a few moments later with a little Gucci suitcase. She pulled out a pale pink jacket with white piping on the collar. 'Mimi loves this. It's very classic, very French.'

Emily held the jacket under Drift's nose. Drift sniffed once and wagged his tail. Then he was off. Jack, Scott, Emily, Bella and even Madame Zelda ran after him as he made directly for the car park at the edge of the common. Drift padded around on the gravel snuffling uncertainly. His ears drooped. The trail seemed to have gone cold.

'Where's Uncle Tony's car?' Bella asked, pointing to a gap between a Mini and an old van.

Emily's suspicious mind was already pulling into the fast lane and speeding towards a crime scene. *Mimi missing. Tony Romaldi missing. Must be a link.* But it seemed she was heading in the wrong direction.

'Tony and Danny were the first to offer to help when they heard me calling for Mimi,' Madame Zelda said, puffing as she caught up with them. 'They said they'd drive around and see if Mimi had wandered off and lost her way. I know Tony's been stirring up trouble lately with his . . .' Madame Zelda hesitated, suddenly remembering there were 'outsiders' present. She gave Bella a meaningful look. 'With his *funny ideas.* But he was very sweet about looking for Mimi. Family always sticks together in crisis. And I'm starting to wonder whether he has a point about the *you-know-what.* How can it have let Mimi be stolen? Someone must have pulled over and *snatched* her. Oh, my poor baby!' She turned and walked forlornly back towards the circus, her fluffy slippers dragging in the grass.

Emily wasn't convinced by the drive-by dognapping theory. How many people would be cruising past Castle Key common first thing on a Sunday morning on the lookout for a stray circus poodle to pinch? There had to be more to it than that. Did someone in the circus have a grudge against Madame Zelda? Was there an age-old feud among the performers? Oh, yes, it was time to draw up a list of suspects and start making enquiries! *We may not have a stolen ruby to investigate,* Emily thought, *but I can work with a stolen poodle instead.* 'Right, we need a planning meeting,' she said, as they walked back across the common. 'Let's get Operation Poodle off the ground.'

'Hang on!' Jack stopped in his tracks. 'We already *had* a plan for this morning. Swimming at the lake? Picnic? Does that ring a bell?'

'Ooh, that sounds cool!' Bella cried. 'Can I come too? I love swimming.'

'Sure,' Scott said. 'But what about your training?'

They all looked up as Luca Romaldi jogged across from the big top, calling to Bella. 'Ah, there you are! Come on, back to work.'

Bella gazed up at her father with big puppy-eyes. 'Daaaaad,' she wheedled, clasping her hands together. 'Emily and the boys have invited me to go swimming at the lake with them. Can I go? Oh, please, please, *please*! I'll do extra practice tomorrow!'

Luca laughed. 'How could I say no to that performance?

Yes, alright. It'll be good for you to have some fun. It's been a tough few days with Gina's accident.'

Bella hugged him. 'I'll go and get my swimming costume,' she said. 'And I'll ask Mum for the rest of that chocolate cake for the picnic.'

'Just one thing before you go,' Luca said. 'Give me your bracelet to look after. He turned to the friends. 'It's a valuable family heirloom and I don't want Bella losing it in the lake or leaving it on the shore where it could be stolen.'

Bella pulled the bracelet from her wrist and almost threw it into her father's hands in her hurry to get going. 'Wait for me!' she called over her shoulder as she sprinted off towards the caravan.

Emily stared at the boys, her pointed chin jutting out in annoyance. 'Er, guys, haven't you *forgotten* something? What about finding Mimi?'

Jack bit his lip and stared at his trainers.

Scott was torn. He could see Emily was upset. But he *really* wanted to go swimming. And how could they tell Bella they'd changed their minds when she came skipping back with her swimming costume? Besides, he knew Jack would be Mr Grumpy all day if he didn't get his picnic. Even Drift was looking up at him, his long pink tongue lolling out – as if to point out it really was very hot and swimming would be lovely and cool. He felt like a referee trying to sort out a disputed penalty in a cup final. He took a deep breath. 'Let's go to the lake just for a couple of hours. We can plan the investigation *while* we have our picnic!'

Emily unclenched her teeth. Scott was right. And, of course, they could look for clues on the way. If Mimi had wandered off, there could be paw-prints. Or they might spot a suspicious car full of dognappers heading for the causeway to the mainland. 'OK,' she said. 'But we'll get straight down to following up leads this afternoon.'

Jack saluted. 'Aye, aye, captain!'

'Let's go and get our bikes,' Scott said as Bella ran back to join them.

'And don't forget the picnic!' Jack added.

Seven

A Dog on a Mission

It was only three miles, but Scott felt as if he'd crossed the Sahara Desert on roller-skates. He had to rub his eyes to check that Polhallow Lake – sparkling like a mirror at the bottom of a shallow valley – was not, in fact, a mirage.

Borrowing a bike for Bella from the equipment store at the circus had *sounded* like a great idea, but it was one Ray and Barbara used for a comedy cycling routine, designed to come apart in the middle and turn into two unicycles as you went along. Even that would have been fine if Ray hadn't forgotten to mention that the catch holding the two halves together was faulty. Jack had valiantly swapped bikes with Bella and then spent the journey attempting to ride the front half as a unicycle while carrying the back half on his head. 'I'm going to work this into my next BMX freestyle competition!' he said, as he crash-landed for the umpteenth time.

And, slowing the pace even more, Emily kept hopping off her bike to examine animal tracks at the side of the road. She'd sent Drift off on the trail of four rabbits, a vole and a discarded burger wrapper. But there'd been no sign of performing pink poodles.

But at last they were parking their bikes on the shore and running towards the old wooden jetty. Bella sprang into the air, tucked into a perfect somersault, flicked her legs straight like the blade of a penknife and entered the water without a ripple. Emily followed with a neat flip.

'Geronimo!' Jack shouted as he and Drift launched themselves in identical heads-up-legs-wheeling belly-flops.

Scott laughed as he ran across the scorching wooden boards and plunged into the deliciously icy water in an athletic racing dive.

The friends swam and splashed and tried to catch tiny fish as they darted through the clear water. Then they sprawled on a warm grassy bank to dry off.

Emily suggested they have their picnic on the tiny tree-covered island in the middle of the lake. 'We could paddle over in kayaks,' she added.

Jack shaded his eyes and scanned the shoreline. 'These would be magical *invisible* kayaks?' he asked.

Emily laughed. 'No, they're in that little boathouse there.' She pointed to a hut nearby. 'It belongs to a friend of my mum and dad. He lets us use the kayaks any time we want.'

The others all thought this was a brilliant idea and soon they were pushing off from the bank in the brightly coloured little boats. Scott took the picnic bags, and Drift squeezed in on Emily's lap. Bella had never paddled a kayak before but she soon got the hang of it. In fact, she was so strong from training for the trapeze act every day that she was the first to reach Willow Island, gliding in under the trailing branches.

Not that it's a race, of course, Jack told himself, gasping for breath as he tried to overtake Bella at the finishing line.

The picnic was soon demolished, right down to Bella's mum's chocolate cake, which had melted to a gooey puddle. 'This is the best day ever,' Bella sighed. 'Thank you for letting me come with you.'

Emily leant against a tree trunk and pulled her notebook from her bag. She wrote OPERATION POODLE on a new page and underlined it twice. But everyone was too full and sleepy to concentrate on the problem of the missing Mimi. Even Emily found her eyelids growing heavy as she listened to the bees bumble and buzz through the long grass. She'd almost dozed off when she suddenly noticed Drift behaving oddly. He kept pricking up his ears into Listening Formation and running to the beach on the other side of the island. Now he was howling like a werewolf. Emily rushed to see what was the matter, just in time to see the little dog leap into the water and start swimming for the far shore of the lake.

Scott, Jack and Bella joined Emily. They gazed across the lake, shielding their eyes against the sun. Drift's dark head could be seen bobbing along as he paddled through the water.

'That's a dog on a mission!' Jack said. 'What's over there? A dog-biscuit factory or something?'

Emily shrugged. 'The North Moors are private land so nobody really goes there. It's all owned by this mega-rich guy called Lord Huddlestone. There's not much up there anyway – just the old disused tin mine and the standing stones.' She pointed into the distance. 'You can see them, there.' Silhouetted against the sun stood several huge slabs of rock, topped with a flat stone, to make what looked like a giant's coffee table.

'I'll have to go after Drift,' Emily said, jogging back towards the kayaks. 'He'll make it to the shore, but I don't know if he'll have the strength to swim back again!'

'We'll come with you,' Scott said. 'There must be *something* over there for Drift to take off like that!'

'Perhaps it's the Beast of the North Moor!' Jack growled, lurching around doing his Beast impression – a strange cross between King Kong and Gollum. 'It prowls the wild moors in search of human flesh . . .'

Bella shuddered.

'Take no notice of Jack!' Scott laughed. 'He can't help it.'

By the time the four friends pulled their kayaks up onto the shingle on the north shore, Drift was barking impatiently. He nudged Emily's hand. Then he trotted a little way and stopped and looked back, head on one side, his spotted ear twitching. You didn't have to be fluent in dog language, Jack thought, to figure out that Drift wanted them to follow him.

Eight

Buried Alive

They'd been sprinting after Drift across the scrubby grass and bracken for some time when Jack began to hear a faint high-pitched whine over the chirping of the grasshoppers and crickets.

'Sounds like an animal in pain,' Bella said, hearing it too.

'It's coming from the standing stones,' Scott panted. 'Look at Drift!'

The little dog had come to a halt and was standing on his hind legs, scratching at one of the upright stones with his front paws.

Emily knelt down next to him. The wailing and whimpering was growing louder and more frantic. 'Something must have fallen down inside the burial chamber beneath the stones.'

'Burial chamber?' Jack echoed. That sounded like something out of a horror movie. He could almost *see* the troubled Stone Age spirits rising from the dead like wisps of fog. The anguished baying sounds coming from within weren't helping much either. He made a mental note to avoid this place on dark and stormy nights! But right now they had a trapped animal to rescue.

There was no entrance to the stones at ground level. They were going to have to climb up and find a way in from the top. *Cool!* Jack thought. He loved rock-climbing. He surveyed the upright slabs. About twice the height of an ordinary door, they leaned inwards at a steep angle. But there should be enough cracks and hollows in the old stone to provide good handholds.

It was a tough climb, but the four friends all managed to scramble up onto the huge flat slab – or *capstone* as Emily called it. They lay on their stomachs on the warm rock to get their breath back. Down on the ground, Drift bounced around on the spot and sent up yips of encouragement.

A section of the capstone had broken away, leaving

a large gap. Scott peered down into the dark interior. Emily handed him a torch. Scott grinned. They'd kayaked across a lake, run over the moors and scaled a vertical rock-face. Only Emily would still have her messenger bag slung over her shoulder with her complete investigation kit inside!

Scott shone the torch down through the gap.

'What can you see?' Jack asked, trying to grab the torch. 'Are there any skeletons down there? Any skulls?'

Scott shook his head. What he *could* see was a wide stone ledge built around the inner surface of the upright slabs about halfway down, and a jumble of large broken rocks and boulders strewn around on the ground below that. He lowered himself through the gap and knelt on the ledge. The whimpering was coming from deep down in a crevice between two big boulders on the ground below. Scott looked down and glimpsed a patch of pale pinky-white in the darkness. His heart thudded. *Was it a body?* Hardly daring to look he directed his torch downwards and peered into the shadows again. The torchlight reflected off two shiny black eyes looking straight back at him.

'It's Mimi!' Bella's voice in Scott's ear made him jump so high he cracked his head on the capstone. He hadn't heard her drop down onto the ledge beside him.

'Look at this!' Bella cried, holding up a rope. One end was attached to the wall. The other end was frayed and shredded. 'She didn't *fall* in here. She's been tied up.'

Emily reached down through the gap and felt the end of the rope. 'It's still soggy.'

Scott nodded. 'I think she was tied up and left on this ledge. She must have chewed through the rope and then tried to jump out through the gap. But she didn't make it and she's fallen down between the stones at the bottom. She's still stuck down there.' He stretched his arm into the crack between the boulders. 'And she's way too far down to reach.'

Mimi howled pitifully.

'It's OK, Mimi, we'll get you out,' Scott said. '*Somehow*,' he added under his breath.

'*Quick thinking and decisive action*, that's how!' Jack called down through the gap. 'You'll have to lower me down there.'

Emily pulled him back by his t-shirt. 'There's no *way* you'd fit into that narrow space between the stones. I'll do it.'

'No, let me!' Bella said. 'I'm the smallest. And I'm used to swinging around upside-down. It's my day job!' Before Emily could protest, Bella had shown Scott the best way to grip her ankles while she slipped over the edge of the ledge like a little snake.

Scott's arms were beginning to shake from holding Bella when she called up to him.

'Hang on, just got to get my hands under . . . yes, OK!'

66

Scott hauled Bella up. She backed onto the ledge and passed a dusty, quivering bundle up through the gap to Emily.

Jack pulled Bella back up through the hole onto the capstone and they exchanged high-fives. 'That was awesome,' he said. 'You were like one of those grabber machines they have in the arcade. Except you actually picked up one of the prizes!'

'Yeah, good work, Bella,' Emily added, laughing as Mimi licked her nose. She cuddled the little dog in her arms. Mimi seemed to be none the worse for her ordeal, although her woolly coat was no longer glossy. It was smeared with dirt and cobwebs.

'So much for all those essential oils!' Scott said, popping his head up through the gap. 'Maybe we should clean her up a bit before we take her back to Madame Zelda.'

The friends climbed down from the burial chamber and carefully lowered Mimi to the ground. Drift seemed shy all of a sudden and hid behind Emily's legs. But Mimi touched her nose to his as if to thank him. Drift batted her shoulder gently with his paw. Together they trotted off back towards the lake, their two tails – one pink with a pom-pom on the end, the other brown and shaggy – wagging in perfect time.

'Uh-oh!' Jack groaned. 'I think *somebody's* in l-u-u-urve!'

They all laughed and ran back to the shore. They

climbed back into the kayaks – with Mimi on Bella's lap – keen to get back to the circus to reunite Mimi with Madame Zelda as quickly as they could.

'We've got to find the monster who tied Mimi up in that chamber,' Emily said, as they paddled back across Polhallow Lake. 'They might as well have buried her alive!'

Scott shook his head. 'They weren't trying to kill her. I found this on the ledge.' He let go of his paddle for a moment, pulled an object from the large side pocket of his swimming shorts and held it out.

Jack stared at it, his forehead scrunched with confusion. 'A plastic cereal bowl?' Am I missing something here?'

'It had water in it,' Scott explained. 'They wouldn't have bothered leaving water unless . . .'

' . . . they planned to go back for her!' Emily finished the sentence. She drew alongside Scott's kayak to take a closer look at the bowl. The white plastic was scratched and chipped with use. On the side was a faded red-and-black-striped logo and the letters ACM.

Things couldn't have worked out better, Emily thought. Coming to the lake had been the right decision, after all. They'd had a lovely swim, rescued Mimi *and* found a top-quality clue to kick-start the investigation. She couldn't wait to get to work, tracking down suspects with the initials ACM.

But Scott was deep in thought as he began paddling again. There was something familiar about that red-

and-black pattern. It was a logo of some kind. And the letters ACM were tugging at his memory too . . . *but where had he seen them before?*

Nine

A Mysterious Appearance

When the friends arrived back at the circus, they found Madame Zelda sitting in front of her caravan clutching one of Mimi's rhinestone collars in her lap.

Bella took her hand. 'Come on! We've got a surprise for you.' She tugged Madam Zelda towards Emily's bike. Mimi was curled up with Drift in the basket on the back. They were both fast asleep. Madame Zelda opened and closed her mouth, not sure whether to laugh or cry. She scooped Mimi up and pressed the little dog to her chest.

'We found her at the standing stones on the North Moor,' Emily explained.

'I can't thank you enough!' Madame Zelda cried, engulfing the friends in huge perfumed hugs. 'When Tony and Danny came back empty-handed I thought I'd never see my little *schmootly-wootly-pie* again.' She rubbed noses with Mimi. 'I should have *known* the ruby would protect her!' In her emotional state, Madame Zelda had forgotten all about keeping the ruby secret from outsiders. 'Losing its powers? *My foot!*' she exclaimed. 'The Eye of Fire sent you four to those standing stones to rescue Mimi. I should never have doubted it!' Madame Zelda kissed Mimi's fur. She wrinkled her nose. 'But I think someone needs a little bath, don't they? With some of those nice rose-scented bubbles . . .'

By now most of the circus had gathered around to welcome Mimi home. There was a whirlwind of thanks and hugs and high-fives. The only person who seemed less than thrilled was Bella's Uncle Tony.

'Isn't it a bit strange that these local kids just *happened* to find Mimi in the middle of nowhere?' he demanded.

'It's a *lot* strange, if you ask me,' Danny chimed in, rolling his massive shot-putter shoulders. 'I bet they're the ones who *stole* her!'

Sylvia Romaldi laughed. 'Don't' be silly, Danny. They were with Bella when they found Mimi.'

Bella looked up at her mum with shining eyes. 'I can't *wait* to tell Gina about this!'

Tony glared at Scott, Jack and Emily. 'Outsiders!' he spat. He turned to Luca. 'You should keep a better eye on the kind of people Bella is running around with. No good will come of it!'

'Yeah,' Danny added. 'Only, like, really *bad* will come of it!'

Luca ignored Danny and gave his older brother a defiant look. '*I'll* be the judge of the company my daughter keeps. And *I* think her new friends are just fine.'

—

Next morning found Jack and Scott, Emily and Drift back at the circus. Bella had asked her parents' permission for her new friends to come and watch the rehearsals. It seemed the entire circus was present apart from Anna Romaldi, the contortionist, who had gone back to her caravan complaining of a headache, and Madame Zelda and Mimi. Much to Drift's disappointment, Madame Zelda had taken Mimi to the vet in Carrickstowe for a check-up after her adventure at the standing stones.

There was so much going on in the big top, it was even more fun than the show itself, Jack thought. Aidan

McDonald, alias the Sword of Persia, was throwing daggers at a special revolving target, while his assistant, Marianne – who, it turned out, was also his wife – belly-danced in front of it. To Jack's delight, Aidan and Marianne let the friends take a turn in front of the board – although Jack was the only one who attempted the belly-dancing part too.

On the other side of the circus ring, Ray and Barbara were working on a new trick. Ray tugged the end of a roll of carpet and Barbara catapulted out like a spinning top, whizzing all over the ring, until she knocked Ray over. Except things weren't quite going to plan. 'You're meant to hit the deck like a *skittle*!' Barbara yelled, jabbing a finger at Ray's stomach – which was as high as she could reach. 'Not a great lump of mashed potato! How did I marry a man who can't even *fall over* properly?'

Meanwhile, the Flying Romaldis were swooping around overhead practising their routine and Mike Turnbull was discussing the sound and light effects for his mind-reading act with one of the technicians. Green lights flashed and snatches of spooky music blared out as they ran through the options.

After an hour the Flying Romaldis took a break and Bella came over to chat, swigging from a bottle of water.

'Can I have a go on the trapeze?' Jack asked.

'Sure,' Bella said. 'You could try a couple of simple moves.' She took him up a ladder to the lowest platform and swung a trapeze bar towards him. 'You just have to jump and catch it.'

Jack grinned and gave a thumbs-up. 'Catch the bar. How hard can it be?' He launched himself into the void. He thought he'd probably be able to fit in a couple of somersaults too. Until he landed on his face in the safety net! He bounced up, watching the empty swing wobbling above his head. 'I'll get it next time!' But he didn't. He tried applying more chalk powder to his hands. It didn't help. He hit the safety net yet again. 'Yeah, not as easy as it looks!' he mumbled as he sat back down.

Scott laughed. 'Gravity three, Jack nil!'

'I can't really *see* you in a sequined leotard anyway,' Emily teased.

Bella was about to get back to work when Enzo Romaldi entered the ring leading Moonlight on a long rein. Jack didn't know anything about horses, but even *he* could see that the majestic white stallion was limping badly. He was about to point it out to the others when suddenly a startled shout rang out from the small platform at the highest point in the big top.

Everyone stopped what they were doing and looked up to see Danny Romaldi swinging by one leg from a safety strap, throwing wild punches around his head like a boxer on the ropes.

'What's up, Dan?' Tony yelled from halfway up a ladder.

'Stupid great seagull just dive-bombed me!' Danny shouted, flipping himself back up onto the platform. 'Must have got in through that hole in the canvas. It's gone now.'

As Scott stared upwards, something about the sight of Danny in his baggy black-and-red tracksuit triggered a fleeting memory. He knew it was something important but – like one of those tiny fish at Polhallow Lake – it darted away before he could catch it. He turned to see whether Jack or Emily had noticed anything, but for some reason they were both staring down into the circus ring as if a spaceship full of little green aliens had just landed there. And they weren't the only ones. Every pair of eyes in the big top was trained on the same spot.

Scott followed their gaze and nearly jumped out of his seat. Sitting cross-legged in the middle of the ring was a figure dressed in a bright red sari. A single spotlight gave her a crimson glow and red smoke curled around her feet. Her face was hidden by swirling veils, but the way she hunched over suggested she was very old. She was as still as a living statue.

'Where did *she* come from?' Jack whispered.

Emily shrugged. 'No idea. She just sort of *appeared*!'

'People don't just appear out of thin air,' Scott snorted. 'We're not in a Harry Potter film, you know!'

Suddenly, the old woman held her hands up as if to demand silence. Rows and rows of shiny gold bangles jangled as they slid down her arms. Her skin was the colour of strong tea.

Confusion rippled round the big top. It was clear nobody had the faintest idea who this mysterious figure was or how she'd got there. Scott looked around for some kind of rope-and-pulley arrangement, or, at the very least, a magic carpet.

'Who are you?' Tony Romaldi demanded. 'And why have you come here?'

The old lady clasped her hands across her stomach. When she spoke, her veil puffed in and out over her mouth. Her voice crackled and rasped but was surprisingly loud.

'My name is Syamantaka!' she proclaimed. 'I have been sent from the Temple of Ganesha to reclaim the cursed ruby . . .'

Ten

The Ruby's Curse

Jack held his breath, waiting for Tony Romaldi to lose his temper. The man had had a hissy fit over three perfectly decent kids helping to find a missing poodle, so he was going to *blow a fuse* at a random old Indian lady pitching up in the middle of the ring and demanding the Romaldis hand over their precious ruby! Even if she *did* claim to have been sent by a god with an elephant's head. But, astonishingly, Tony kept his hair on. He even took a step back. Meanwhile, Enzo Romaldi handed Moonlight's reins to the Sword of Persia and addressed the old woman.

'There has clearly been a mistake,' he explained in a confident tone. 'The Romaldi family ruby is *not* cursed! It was given to our ancestor by a maharajah. The Eye of Fire *protects* us from harm.'

Syamantaka shook her head slowly and raised her hands like a conductor controlling an orchestra. 'Enzo Romaldi! The Eye of Fire did not belong to the maharajah to give away. He and his family were merely the earthly guardians of the ruby on behalf of the Temple of Ganesha. As long as the maharajah's family was still in existence, it was theirs to entrust to you as they wished, and the protective powers were transferred to your family – that much is true. But since the last member of the maharajah's family died without an heir, the conditions of that gift no longer apply. The Eye of Fire now bestows a terrible curse upon you as long as it remains in your possession . . .'

Tony Romaldi stepped up. 'Tell us, O Wise One! When exactly did she die?'

'O Wise One?' Jack sniggered. 'Does he think he's in the Bible or something?'

'Shhh!' Emily hissed. 'I'm trying to listen.'

The old woman waved her hands above her head. 'The last surviving member of the dynasty was an old, old woman. She drew her last breath on Friday . . .'

Tony gasped and staggered as if he'd been thumped on the nose. '*Friday!* That was the night of Gina's accident.'

Fear flickered across the faces of the Romaldi family who were now all gathered around the old lady.

Emily longed to jot down some notes. Something Tony had said was puzzling her. But she was afraid of drawing attention by rummaging in her shoulder bag for her notebook. She had a feeling this was *not* the kind of family gathering where Tony Romaldi would welcome outsiders.

'And how can we lift the curse?' Enzo Romaldi demanded.

Syamantaka rose to her feet. In her long robes it was almost as if she were hovering above the ground. 'The Eye of Fire,' she chanted, 'must be returned to its rightful place as the third eye in the great statue of Ganesha in the sacred temple.'

'You mean we have to take it back to India?' Luca Romaldi asked. 'But we don't even know where this temple is.'

'That is precisely why I am here! Ganesha is grateful to you for safeguarding the ruby. He does not wish to punish you. I will arrange for the ruby to be returned and your family will be freed from the curse of the Eye of Fire!'

'Oh, yeah, and what if we don't *want* to give it back?' Barbara marched across the ring and glared at the veiled figure. 'What are you going to do about it?'

'Zip it, Barb!' Ray snapped, pulling her back. 'Don't you go sticking your oar in.'

Barbara batted Ray's hands away. 'I'm a Romaldi too. At least I *was* until I married you. You keep your great big hooter out!'

Syamantaka held her hands up for silence again. 'Should you decide *not* to return the Eye of Fire, misfortune will continue to befall the Romaldi family until everything you have ever worked for lies in *ruins* . . .' She made the word *ruins* last a long time.

Emily felt a shiver run down her spine. *I'm not even a Romaldi and this woman's giving me the creeps.* She glanced at Bella, standing at the edge of the ring. Her dark eyes were so wide she looked like a bush-baby.

'Forgive me for asking,' Luca Romaldi said. 'But how do we know you are genuine?'

Syamantaka pulled an envelope from her robes and handed it to Enzo. 'This document from the Indian Board of Cultural Affairs confirms all I have told you. I will return at the same time tomorrow to hear your decision and collect the ruby.' And with that she swept out of the big top with a rustle of her sari and a swish of her veils.

As soon as she'd gone, the Romaldis crowded around Enzo to look at the letter.

'I told you that ruby wasn't protecting us any more!' Tony slapped the letter with the back of his hand. 'It's all here in black and white. Now do you believe me? We have to get rid of it.'

Luca took the letter and held it up to the light as if checking a twenty-pound note for a watermark. 'I'm not sure about all this.'

'Too right!' Barbara agreed. 'Some old woman turns up in a puff of smoke, waving a bit of paper around, and we're supposed to hand over a priceless ruby?'

Enzo commanded everyone to be quiet. He smoothed his white moustache and shook his head sadly. 'If you remember the words of the legend, the maharajah gave the Eye of Fire to our ancestor for *safe-keeping*, not to own for eternity. And it is also true that we have suffered a string of misfortunes since Friday: Gina's accident, a pole breaking which could have caused Barbara a serious injury, Mimi going missing. And just this morning,' he added, 'Moonlight has gone lame.' He patted the stallion's neck. 'As head of the family, I need time to think about the best course of action. But it seems we may be dealing with a force beyond our control.'

'Come on!' Emily whispered, pulling the boys with her. 'Let's go before Tony remembers we're here and blames *us* for the ruby's curse!'

There was a new mystery to solve and Emily couldn't wait to get started.

Eleven

It All Fits Perfectly!

A force beyond our control. Scott turned the phrase over in his mind as the friends slipped out of the big top and meandered down to the harbour. Whatever *force* was at work, Scott wasn't going to start believing in cursed jewels. This was the twenty-first century after all!

They sat down on the harbour wall and gazed out at the fishing boats.

Jack pulled his t-shirt over his face. 'I come on behalf of the Temple of Ganesha,' he chanted. 'The ruby is *cu-u-u-u-ursed* . . .' He pulled down his shirt and stared at Scott and Emily, bugging his big blue eyes at them. 'Now, would someone mind explaining what, precisely, *that* was all about?'

Emily laughed. But then she grabbed her notebook and began to scribble furiously. When she looked up, Scott recognized the glint of excitement in her eyes. She was on to something.

'So, did either of you notice anything *strange* when Tony was talking to Syamantaka?' Emily demanded.

'Hmm, let me see,' Jack murmured, stroking his chin as if deep in thought. '*Apart* from the mysterious Indian lady appearing out of nowhere in a puff of smoke, you mean?' He grinned and shook his head. 'Nope, it all seemed like a pretty average morning at the circus to me. You notice anything, Scott?'

Emily sighed impatiently. 'Remember when Syamantaka told them about the last member of the maharajah's family dying? Well, Tony jumped in straight away and asked, "When did she die?"'

Jack and Scott looked at each other with blank faces.

'When did *she* die?' Emily repeated, bouncing her pen up and down on her notebook. 'Think about it! How did Tony know it was a woman?'

'Well, he had a fifty-fifty chance of being right . . .' Scott ventured.

Emily nodded. 'But it didn't sound as if he was *guessing*. And wouldn't he have been more likely to say "he" if he didn't know it was a woman? *I* think Tony Romaldi knows a lot more about this Syamantaka lady than he was letting on! I *knew* I should never have crossed out Operation Ruby.' Emily wrote the title again at the top of a new page. 'Oh, yes,' she murmured happily. 'We're back in business!'

'You don't think Tony could be running some kind of jewel-smuggling operation, do you?' Scott asked seriously.

'Of course, that could be it!' Emily breathed. 'Syamantaka is his contact in India!' Then she realized Scott was teasing. She knew Scott and Jack thought she was *obsessed* with smuggling. She gave Scott a good shove. He fell off the harbour wall and rolled onto the pebbly beach. Drift pounced on him. This looked like a great game!

'*Someone* is trying to get their hands on that ruby,' Emily said, ignoring Scott and Drift wrestling at her feet. 'And I'm sure it's not the Indian Board of Cultural Affairs, *or* the god Ganesha, for that matter. It's Tony Romaldi. He's been trying to get the family to sell the Eye of Fire for ages, but nobody's been listening.'

'Apart from his trusty sidekick, Danny Boy,' Jack pointed out.

Emily nodded. 'I'm sure they're behind this whole *curse* thing. We just need to figure out how . . .'

'Whoah!' Jack said, holding up both hands. 'Hold it right there!'

'What?' Emily asked excitedly. Just occasionally, in amongst the jokes, Jack came up with a truly genius idea. Had he come up with a breakthrough again?

'If there's *figuring out* to be done, I need lunch first.' Jack tapped his forehead. 'A finely-tuned instrument like this doesn't run on empty, you know!'

Emily groaned. *Like I said*, she thought, *just occasionally . . .*

Scott sat up on the beach and looked at his watch. 'It is nearly lunchtime, I suppose. Let's go to Dotty's and continue this investigation over bacon sandwiches.'

'Now you're talking!' Jack high-fived his brother and took off down the road. Drift was right behind him. *Bacon* was another of his favourite words!

—

The friends settled down at a table outside Dotty's Tea Rooms on the seafront.

'This is more like it!' Jack announced, pouring ketchup onto his sandwich.

'So, what are you thinking, Em?' Scott looked around to make sure no one was listening in. 'That Tony Romaldi paid this Syamantaka woman to turn up and start banging on about curses?'

Emily nodded and skimmed through the notes in her

book. 'Yeah. That's my theory. He thinks it'll persuade the family to hand over the ruby to get rid of all the bad luck they've been having . . .'

'But when they give the ruby to Syamantaka tomorrow it's not going back to India, is it?' Scott continued. 'She'll nip round the back of the big top and hand it over to good old Tony.'

'Exactly!' Emily said. 'I bet a million pounds that the so-called letter from the Indian Cultural Affairs people is a total fake.'

'Hang on a minute,' Jack mumbled through a mouthful of bacon. 'Aren't you guys forgetting one *minor* point?'

Emily and Scott stared at him. Drift stared at him too, but only because he was tracking the sandwich in Jack's hand. In Drift's mind, bacon was far more interesting than rubies. Normally Jack would've been inclined to agree. But right now he'd spotted a fatal flaw in Scott and Emily's logic.

'What are you on about?' Scott asked.

Jack fed a piece of bacon to Drift and gave a knowing smile. 'Well, if this whole cursed ruby deal has just been made up by Tony, how come the Romaldis have been having all these accidents? After all, if *I* hadn't shown up, things would have been even worse!'

Scott nearly choked on his banana milkshake. 'Excuse me, Lone Ranger, we all found Mimi together, remember?'

Drift pricked up his ears. Did someone say *Mimi*?

'I'm just saying,' Jack explained, 'that there's been a lot of *dodgy* stuff happening. And now Moonlight's mysteriously gone lame as well . . .'

Scott rolled his eyes. 'But a *curse*? You'll be telling me you believe in the Tooth Fairy next!'

Jack dropped his jaw in mock horror. 'You're telling me there's no such thing as the Tooth Fairy? Who left all that money under my pillow then?'

Emily ignored the boys. She'd just had a genius idea of her own. 'What if Tony Romaldi set all those accidents up to make it *look* like there was a curse? To make the story more believable?'

Jack gulped. 'You think Danny deliberately dropped Gina so she head-planted off the trapeze?' He shook his head and whistled. 'But Gina's Tony's *niece*. She's Danny's *cousin*. I know Danny's not exactly Mr Personality, but that would be pure *evil*!'

But Scott was on the same wavelength as Emily. 'Maybe Tony and Danny didn't *mean* the accident to be that bad. Remember Gina said she'd have fallen into the safety net if she hadn't grabbed for that other swing. Perhaps the accident was supposed to be more an embarrassment than . . .'

' . . . than a fatal spinal injury?' Jack snorted. He still wasn't buying it. 'And what about Mimi? Madame Zelda said Tony and Danny were the first to go off looking for her!'

Under the table, Drift was getting worried. Why did

everyone keep saying *Mimi*? Was she in trouble again?

Meanwhile, Emily was studying her notes and chewing on her pencil. She was sure that Tony and Danny had dognapped Mimi, but Jack had a point. Then it came to her! 'What if Tony's wife Anna is in on the scheme too? She could have grabbed Mimi from outside the caravan while Madame Zelda went inside to make that special tea. Then she stuffed Mimi in the boot of their car. Meanwhile, Tony and Danny are waiting just round the corner to make sure they're the first on the scene when Madame Zelda raises the alarm. They form a search party and zoom off in the car.'

'Only they're *not* looking for Mimi at all,' Scott added. 'She's locked in the boot. They're *looking* for a good place to hide her away for a day or two. They don't actually want to hurt her so they leave her a bowl of water. They just want to cause a big upset.'

'It all fits perfectly,' Emily said. Then she shook her head sadly. 'It's just a shame we can't *prove* any of this.'

Suddenly Scott leaped up. He stood on the wall and punched the air with both fists, sending a group of startled seagulls flapping into the air. 'Oh, yes, we can! Quick, Em, have you still got that bowl we found when we rescued Mimi?'

'Sure. I put it in my bag when we got back from the lake.' Emily handed the bowl to Scott. 'I've already checked it for fingerprints,' she told the boys. 'There's nothing. Mimi must have licked them all off. And I've been racking my brains to think whose initials could be ACM. Of course, there's Aidan McDonald, but why would the Sword of Persia have anything to do with all this?'

'Tony could be short for Anthony or Antonio,' Jack suggested. 'That would explain the A. But even with my lousy spelling, I know Romaldi doesn't start with an M . . .'

Scott grinned. 'You're both barking up the wrong tree. I *knew* I'd seen this logo before – an oval with black and red stripes and a red cross. I'd have twigged sooner if half of it wasn't scraped off! It's AC Milan!'

'AC Milan?' Jack and Emily chorused.

'Yeah. Football club. Italian. They've won more world titles than any other team . . .'

'I *know* who AC Milan are!' Jack snapped. 'But how does it tell us that Danny and Tony were the ones who nabbed Mimi? You're not suggesting they play in the Italian league in their spare time?'

'No,' Scott said. 'But they *support* AC Milan. At least Danny does. I *knew* there was a connection when I saw him in the big top this morning, but I couldn't put my finger on it. He was wearing an AC Milan tracksuit. And this bowl must be part of a souvenir breakfast set or something. I'm sure it's Danny's.'

'Brilliant!' Emily said, writing in her notebook. 'This definitely puts Tony and Danny in the frame for Mimi's disappearance as well as Gina's accident . . .'

Drift could bear it no longer. They *kept* talking about Mimi. She must be in trouble again! He shot out from under the table. Straight into the path of a speeding bicycle.

Twelve

Rock Solid Proof

There was a screech of brakes and a blare of horns. 'Oh, no!' Jack groaned. The bicycle bore the unmistakable hunched figure of his arch enemy: local cleaning lady and mega-busybody, Mrs Irene Loveday. She was working her usual fashion statement of orange high-visibility jacket, blue checked apron and flowery dress. Her pink trainers matched the bike helmet perched on her grey curls.

'Oh, I'm so sorry!' Emily spluttered, snatching Drift up into her arms. 'I don't know *why* Drift darted out like that.'

Mrs Loveday patted herself down as if checking for broken bones. 'It's bad enough with all these circus types wandering around, without *dogs* running out of control. There was even a funny little man here reading peoples' minds yesterday,' she went on without pausing for breath. 'I said to Dotty, "I've only popped in for a Chelsea Bun. I'm not stopping here to have *my* mind boggled into a Neurotic Trance."'

'Er, *hypnotic* trance?' Emily asked. Mrs Loveday was famous for mixing up her words.

'Is *that* what they're calling it these days?' Mrs Loveday said doubtfully. 'Well, I turned round and went home for a custard cream instead.'

Jack tried to keep his laughter from bubbling over – even though he felt as if a hysterical hyena was trapped inside his body. *You don't need to be a mind-reader,* Jack thought, *to know what Mrs Loveday's thinking. She spends the whole day informing everyone.* Suddenly he had an idea. 'You haven't come across an old Indian lady dressed all in red, have you?' He did his best to sound polite, especially as he knew that Mrs Loveday considered him to be lower down the food chain than plankton.

Mrs Loveday narrowed her eyes and glared at Jack. '*Red Indians*? This isn't the *Wild West,* you know. It must be a Pigment of your Imagination!'

'A *figment*, you mean,' Scott murmured.

'Exactly!' Mrs Loveday said. 'And your brother has far too many *figments* for his own good!'

Jack tried not to make matters worse by laughing again. He looked at Scott and Emily. Appearing out of nowhere in a puff of smoke was impressive enough. But setting foot in Castle Key without registering on Mrs Loveday's Gossip Radar really *was* a mystery!

—

The friends met at Stone Cottage the next morning and set off for the circus. The plan was simple. They would establish observation posts and keep watch on all possible entrances to the big top. When Syamantaka returned, they would be there to witness her arrival.

'I looked up *Syamantaka* on the internet last night,' Scott told Emily on the way. 'Guess what? It's the name of the famous jewel of the Sun God in Indian mythology – a ruby with great powers.'

'Spooky!' Jack said. 'So maybe our lady really *is* on a mission from the Temple of Ganesha?'

But Emily wasn't convinced. 'Tony could easily have found that information on the internet too. No doubt he told her to use that name when he hired her to play the part. He probably thought it would sound more authentic.'

At the circus it seemed that everyone – not just the

Romaldi family – was gathered inside the big top, awaiting the second coming of the mysterious Indian lady.

'If anyone asks why you're here, just say you're searching for a watch you dropped yesterday,' Emily told the boys. 'Drift and I will take the fire exit at the back.'

Jack grinned and saluted. 'Aye, aye, captain. I'll take the main entrance.'

Scott watched Jack saunter off looking fixedly at his feet – doing a very bad imitation of someone searching for a lost watch. He couldn't have looked more suspicious if he'd had a machine-gun sticking out of his back pocket.

Scott positioned himself near a side entrance that gave access to the wings. He found a little split in the canvas and peeped through. The Romaldis were gathered at the edge of the ring, chatting nervously. Enzo, Luca, Tony and Danny were huddled together, locked in a heated argument. Scott wished he could hear what they were saying. Suddenly, Tony glanced across to Anna Romaldi, who was talking to Bella's mum, Sylvia. Anna grimaced and rubbed her temples with her fingertips. When she spoke, Scott could lip-read the words, *headache* and *lie down*. Sylvia offered to go with her but Anna shook her head and hurried away.

Where's she going? Scott wondered. He didn't have to wait long to find out. Moments later, Anna Romaldi emerged from the big top through the side entrance. She paused and ran a hand through her thick blonde hair, her eyes flicking left and right. But instead of heading towards her caravan, she scurried off round the back of the big top. Scott waited a moment, then followed. He peeped round the curve of the tent. There was nobody there. Anna Romaldi had vanished!

Scott felt the side of the big top for an opening in the canvas. But all he could find was a small flap at the bottom. He lifted the corner and saw part of a low wooden structure. He realized it was the edge of the circus ring – which was raised about a metre off the ground on wooden staging. He looked closer. There was a small hole in the side. Had Anna squeezed through and crawled *under* the circus ring?

Scott decided to take a look. With a lot of writhing and twisting he squashed through the gap and found himself in a low dark space. He noticed a light moving around and began to commando crawl towards it, weaving through the wooden struts and posts that supported the circus ring. He could hear footsteps overhead. This must be how it felt to be a mouse creeping around under the floorboards. He bit back curses as his head bumped against hinges and handles sticking out from various hatches and trapdoors set into the underside of the ring.

The light up ahead stopped moving. With his muscles cramping and his neck aching, Scott inched towards it. At last he saw Anna's blonde hair in the light of a torch hanging from a hook on a beam. At first he couldn't figure out what she was doing. Then he glimpsed a flash of red satin. She was wriggling into a sari like a snake shedding its skin in reverse. Scott watched in amazement as Anna twisted around in the low, confined space. She wasn't a contortionist for nothing! Her body seemed to contain no bones at all. At the same time, Anna was somehow managing to dab a dark liquid on her arms and hands. The chemical tang of the stage make-up cut through the smell of damp grass and wood under the ring. A few more seconds and she'd added a dark wig, gold bangles and several veils.

Scott just had time to snap a photo on his mobile phone. Then, in a single move, Anna turned off the torch, slid open a hatch above her head, and sprang up into the circus ring in a cloud of red smoke.

Scott heard something drop and roll across the grass. He picked it up and read the label by the light of his phone. It was a small canister of red stage smoke.

Anna Romaldi – a.k.a. Anna-lastica the contortionist – had transformed into Syamantaka!

Scott spun round on his stomach and crawled back as fast as his weary knees and elbows would propel him. He couldn't wait to show Emily and Jack the photo. This was rock solid proof that Syamantaka was a fake.

But when Scott finally reached the edge of the ring and wriggled out through the gap, he found he'd lost his bearings. This wasn't the same hole he'd entered by.

Instead of being outside in the fresh air and sunshine at the back of the big top, he'd emerged into a partitioned-off area stuffed with racks of costumes and boxes of mats and hoops and poles and juggling clubs and stilts. He recognized it from Bella's grand tour of the circus: he was in the wings at the side of the circus ring.

'What d'you think *you're* doing, mate?' asked a menacing voice.

Scott whipped round to see Danny Romaldi standing in the doorway, with a grin on his face and a mighty curved sword in his hand.

Thirteen

Playing with Fire

What do I think I'm doing?

Scott tried to think of a good answer. *Spying on your mum* probably wasn't the best reply to give a guy with a scimitar in his hand. The blade was massive, shiny and looked terrifyingly sharp. Danny must have been raiding the Sword of Persia's supplies.

But it seemed Danny wasn't terribly interested in answers anyway. He launched himself at Scott like a ninja.

Scott grabbed the first thing that came to hand from the nearest box of props – a plastic Aladdin's lamp – and lunged at Danny's legs in a flying tackle that would have earned him an instant red card on the football pitch. The scimitar flashed through the air and sliced down towards Scott's arm.

He closed his eyes and waited for the pain to start.

The lamp took the impact. The scimitar bounced off and flew out of Danny's hand. Scott opened his eyes and almost laughed with relief. It wasn't a real sword! It must be a prop from one of the other acts. And that tackle had taken Danny's legs out from under him. His arms windmilled and he crashed to the ground with a thud.

Scott was heading for the exit when he heard Danny clambering to his feet. He turned to see Danny lower his head and charge. Scott dodged at the last moment like a matador in a bullring and Danny barrelled into a rack of costumes. But he was straight back up again, snatching away a pink scarf that had wrapped itself round his face.

Before Scott could make another move, Danny grabbed hold of a rope hanging from a tent-pole and swung out. He let out a mighty roar as his feet struck Scott's chest and sent him staggering backwards into a snake-charmer's basket. As Scott tried to climb out of the basket, he smelled burning. Danny was down from the rope and lighting a fire-juggling torch!

'Got you now, you little loser!' Danny Romaldi yelled, his snarling face lit up by the flare of the torch.

Scott struggled to free himself. But he was folded double and wedged firmly in the basket. Danny moved towards him.

＊

Meanwhile, outside the big top, Emily just couldn't understand it: she and Drift were highly experienced Undercover Surveillance Operatives, and they'd both had their eyes peeled, but neither of them had seen a mysterious old Indian lady approach. Drift's ears hadn't so much as *twitched*. Nor had Jack or Scott raised the alarm from their vantage points around the tent. And yet, in a flash of light and a cloud of smoke, Syamantaka had suddenly appeared in the middle of the circus ring, just as she had done yesterday. If Emily hadn't been peeping in through the fire exit and seen it with her own eyes, she wouldn't have believed it possible.

Now the old lady was addressing the Romaldi family as they gathered around her. 'What is your decision?' she demanded. 'Do you agree to return the Eye of Fire to India and lift the curse from your family?'

Enzo Romaldi stepped forward. The proud old man seemed to have aged overnight. His back was bent and his white moustache drooped. Emily guessed he and the rest of the family had been up all night talking over the options. 'We have considered your words carefully,' he said. 'We believe that you speak the truth, Syamantaka. The ruby *is* cursed. Our family has never known a string of misfortunes such as this. Moonlight is still lame, Tony's wife Anna has been plagued with headaches, and only this morning the engine of our main storage truck has seized up. Therefore, we must . . .' Enzo's voice faded to a whisper. He couldn't bring himself to say the words.

Tony stepped forward and finished the sentence. 'We must entrust the Eye of Fire to your care, Syamantaka, and allow you to return it to its rightful home in India, so that the curse will end.'

Syamantaka raised her hands and wisps of red smoke curled from her sleeves. 'The Romaldi family has chosen wisely. So be it!'

Emily ground her teeth. Her heart felt as heavy as a lump of concrete. *This wasn't right!* The family were walking straight into a trap and Tony was going to get his hands on the ruby. And now the Romaldis were leaving the big top with Syamantaka. No doubt they were heading for Enzo's caravan to unlock the casket for the very last time.

On the other side of the big top Jack ducked out of sight behind an empty hotdog stand as the Romaldis trooped out through the main entrance. He'd been watching Syamantaka's performance too. He had to admit, the whole magical appearance routine was pretty convincing. Between them, he and Scott and Emily had *all* the entrances covered; the old lady must have had an invisibility cloak or an invisibility *sari* or something to have snuck past them.

Jack ran round the outside of the big top to look for Scott. But when he came to the entrance to the wings, there was nobody there. Scott must have headed for Enzo Romaldi's caravan already. Jack was turning back when he heard something that sounded like Tarzan swinging through the jungle.

'Ahhhhh-ahhhh!' The cry had come from inside the wings. He paused and listened. There was a thud and a crash and a muffled cry.

That sounded very much like Trouble with a capital T!

Jack pulled back the canvas and peeped into the wings. It took a moment for his brain to work out what his eyes were seeing. Danny Romaldi was waving a burning torch above his head. Meanwhile, Scott appeared to be sitting in a laundry basket. His head, feet and hands were poking out of the top and he was rocking the basket from side to side. He was clearly stuck fast. Now Danny was running towards Scott holding the torch aloft like the Olympic flame. It seemed he'd mistaken Scott for a disposable barbecue and was planning to set light to him.

'Oh, no, you don't!' Jack yelled, as he leaped onto Danny's back and grabbed the arm brandishing the torch.

Danny threw his head back and shook Jack off. But at that moment, Scott finally succeeded in toppling the basket over and he was now rolling across the matting. The basket powered into Danny's knees like a bowling ball. Danny keeled over. There was a clang as his head bounced off a tent-pole and he landed, winded and dazed, with Jack sitting on top of him. Jack prised the torch from Danny's hand and held it up like a trophy.

'Strike!' Scott shouted.

'Ah, yes, the old Basket Roll Move!' Jack laughed. 'Works every time.'

'A little help here, please?' Scott was still wobbling round in circles trying to extract himself from the basket.

Jack gave the basket a little push with his foot. 'What about *Thanks-for-saving-my-life-Jack* first? Without my *quick thinking and decisive action* you'd have been grilled to medium-rare by now!'

'Yeah, cheers for that,' Scott mumbled.

Jack took Scott's hand and helped free him from the basket. Scott sat down next to Jack to help pin down Danny who was starting to thrash about, groaning and spitting out threats.

'We'll have to tie him up.' Scott reached for the pink scarf that was lying on the floor.

'You shouldn't play with fire, mate,' Jack told Danny as they bound his wrists to a tent-pole. 'Didn't your mum tell you it's dangerous?'

'*His* mum's far too busy impersonating mysterious old Indian ladies,' Scott said. Then he told Jack how he'd seen Anna change into her Syamantaka disguise and pop up through the trapdoor.

Jack pulled the last knot tight around Danny's wrists and looked at Scott. 'The Romaldis have just agreed to give Syamantaka the ruby. They're heading over to Enzo's caravan to get it out of the casket now. We've got to stop them before it's too late!'

Fourteen

More Shocks for the Romaldi Family

Emily peeped in through the window of Enzo
Romaldi's caravan.

Syamantaka was sitting cross-legged on the sofa,
swathed in her red sari and veils. She was chanting softly
with her hands together as if in prayer. The Romaldi
family looked on in gloomy silence as Enzo pulled
back the curtain that concealed the carved casket.
Barbara kept clenching her fists. Ray stood behind her,

his huge hands gripping her shoulders as if to restrain her from decking Syamantaka with a swift upper-cut. Madame Zelda was fanning herself with a handkerchief and clutching Mimi to her bosom. Bella perched on the edge of a chair next to her parents, while Tony Romaldi hovered by the door.

Two people were missing. Emily had seen Anna slip out of the big top complaining of a headache – but Scott had that exit covered and surely he would have reported by now if she'd been up to something. She must still be lying down in her own caravan. As for Danny, he must have peeled off from the group as they all filed out of the big top. Emily had a feeling that he was up to no good but she couldn't go looking for him now. *Where are Scott and Jack when I need them?* she wondered. They couldn't have picked a worse time to disappear.

Enzo Romaldi was beckoning for Bella and Luca to step up to the casket. *Poor Bella!* Emily thought. There were dark rings under her eyes and her hands trembled as she unhooked the little silver key from her charm bracelet.

Emily's instincts all told her she should storm into the caravan and shout, 'Don't give her the ruby!' But she had no *proof* that Syamantaka was a fake. All they had was the AC Milan water bowl connecting Danny to Mimi's disappearance. That was hardly enough to base an entire case on. For once, Emily wasn't sure what to do. She and Drift had carried out their investigations alone for years before Jack and Scott came to stay in Castle Key this summer, but now – and Emily could hardly believe she was even thinking this – she realized she'd come to rely on Scott's clear-thinking and Jack's courage. Courage that often bordered on *insanity*, it was true, but she could use some of it right now.

Luca was flipping open the back of his watch and sliding out his key. *I've got to do something,* Emily thought. 'Find the boys!' she whispered to Drift. 'Fetch Scott and Jack.' The little dog hared back towards the big top. Emily watched him for a second, then picked up a stick from the grass and banged it against the side of the caravan. It wasn't exactly the *classiest* distraction in the world, but it might just buy some time.

She rolled under the caravan and cowered behind a wheel as she heard the door bang open. She could see feet and legs and then Tony's upside-down face as he looked underneath the caravan. Emily held her breath and closed her eyes waiting for a hand to reach in and drag her out. But at long last, Tony stood up again.

'Nothing there! Must have been the wind,' he said.

Emily listened to the family clattering back inside. She crawled out and looked through the window. Enzo, Luca and Bella were huddled around the casket once more, about to insert their silver keys into the locks. Oh, no, it was too late . . .

Suddenly Emily heard a bark. She turned to see Drift running towards her, followed by Jack and Scott. She flew to meet them. 'Where *were* you two?' she cried, picking Drift up and hugging him tight.

'Rescuing Scott from being chargrilled by Danny Boy!' Jack panted.

'The Romaldis are in Enzo's caravan about to hand over the ruby!' Emily gasped. 'We've got to *do* something!'

'I've got proof Symantaka is a fake!' Scott grabbed Emily by the hand and pulled her towards the caravan. Jack and Drift were right behind them.

The friends took the steps in a single bound and threw open the door. 'Stop!' Scott yelled.

'Who do you think you are?' Tony Romaldi roared. 'Barging in on a private family meeting like this!'

Slowly, Enzo Romaldi took his key from the keyhole and looked from Scott to Tony and then back to Scott again.

Suddenly there was a wail from the sofa. Syamantaka was swaying and waving her arms around in an alarming way. 'The outsiders must leave!' she warbled. 'Otherwise the curse of the Eye of Fire will rain down upon you . . . Its vengeance will be terrible to behold . . .'

'You heard the lady!' Tony yelled. 'I'll soon get rid of this rabble.' He grabbed Scott by the scruff of his t-shirt.

'Let him go!' Bella shouted. 'These are my friends.'

'Wait!' Luca Romaldi put his arm around his daughter. 'Bella's right. These young people have helped us before.

They deserve a chance to explain themselves.'

Enzo Romaldi nodded. 'Please explain the meaning of this intrusion.'

Scott shook away Tony's grip and stepped forward. 'We've come to stop you giving the ruby away. The Eye of Fire *isn't* cursed. Tony and Danny and Anna have staged all the accidents. And I have proof . . .' Scott reached into the pocket of his jeans for his phone, so he could show them the all-important photo. But his phone wasn't there. He checked his other pocket. *No phone!* Scott's stomach turned inside out.

No phone, no proof!

'Very funny!' Tony blustered. 'Nobody believes your silly little fairy tales!'

'If it's a *fairy tale*, explain *this*!' Jack didn't let a minor detail like the missing proof bother him. He shouldered past Scott and lunged at Syamantaka. He grabbed a handful of veils and tugged. The black wig came away in his hand too, revealing the blonde hair beneath.

'*Anna!*' Enzo Romaldi gasped.

'*Anna!*' Emily breathed, just as astonished.

Anna sank her head into her brown-painted hands.

The stunned silence was broken by Danny Romaldi stumbling into the caravan. 'Dad, Dad! You'll never believe it!' he panted. 'Those two brothers hit me over the head and tied me up!' Suddenly he noticed that his attackers were right in front of his nose. 'Yeah, *those* two!' he blurted, pointing a stubby finger at Scott and

Jack. 'Ambushed me from behind. They know about . . .'

'Shut up, Danny!' Tony, Enzo and Luca shouted in unison.

Suddenly everyone was talking at the same time. Enzo clapped his hands three times. 'Quiet, please!' The hubbub ceased. He turned to Tony. 'What do you have to say for yourself?' The old man's voice trembled with barely-controlled anger. 'Have you been playing a *trick* on us?'

Tony shrugged. 'OK, it's true.' He glared around the room. 'We *wanted* everyone to think the ruby was cursed.'

Luca shook his head at his brother in disbelief. 'You staged Gina's accident?'

Bella pummelled Danny's chest with her fists. 'You dropped Gina on purpose! How *could* you?'

Luca pulled her gently away, although he was looking at Danny as if he'd like to use him as a punch-bag too.

Danny folded his arms sulkily. 'She wasn't *meant* to fall past the safety net. That was her *own* stupid fault!'

'And they tied Mimi up in the standing stones,' Emily said, taking the AC Milan bowl from her bag and handing it to Danny. 'I think this is yours.'

'You *monsters!*' Madame Zelda cried. 'Poor Mimi's been having nightmares ever since.'

At the mention of his new friend, Drift trotted over and touched noses with Mimi who was curled up on Madame Zelda's lap. Nobody was going to lay a finger on her again if *he* had anything to do with it!

116

Enzo regarded Tony with disappointment in his eyes. 'And no doubt you sabotaged the pole that snapped, and put the nail in Moonlight's shoe, and the sugar in the truck's petrol tank . . .'

'But *why* did you do it, Tony?' Sylvia Romaldi asked.

'It was for the sake of the family, if you must know!' Tony said in a hurt tone – as if he'd been running some heroic undercover mission that no one else had been brave enough to attempt. 'The letter I showed you was genuine. It came a few weeks ago. The maharajah's last descendant really *has* died and the Indian Board of Cultural Affairs want the ruby to be returned to the Temple of Ganesha. They're offering us a measly few thousand pounds . . .' Tony pulled the letter from his pocket and read aloud. '. . . *as a token of our nation's gratitude for the safe-keeping of this cultural treasure . . .*'

'So, why didn't you just tell us instead of causing all those "accidents"?' Barbara yelled.

Tony rolled his eyes. 'I knew if I told you the truth you would just hand the ruby over to them like a bunch of suckers! *Our* ruby! But I thought that if you could see that the ruby wasn't protecting us any more, you'd agree to sell it instead. We deserve more than a few thousand—'

'Yeah!' Danny interrupted. 'That jeweller we asked in London told us it was worth *millions* . . .'

'*Not* that we were planning to *sell* the Eye of Fire ourselves, of course!' Tony cut in sharply, glaring at

Danny. 'We enquired purely for *insurance purposes . . .*'

'And what about Anna's Indian mystic lady impression?' Sylvia Romaldi demanded.

Tony sighed like a teacher disappointed that his class wasn't keeping up. 'Since you lot refused to believe that the accidents meant that the ruby had lost its protective power, we had to go one step further. Symantaka's appearance was supposed to convince you that the ruby was actually *cursed* and *causing* the accidents. We thought that would persuade you to hand it over.' He looked at his father and smiled. 'Once you'd given the ruby to Anna we were just planning to keep it safe until you all saw sense and we could sell it together, for the good of the family business . . .'

Luca shook his head sadly. 'I'm afraid I don't believe you, Tony.'

There was a murmur of agreement from everyone in the room.

Finally Enzo spoke. 'Tony, it's clear to all of us that you and Anna and Danny were going to go off by yourselves and sell the ruby and keep the proceeds. If you were as concerned about the family as you claim to be, you'd hardly be planning to leave us at the end of the season! Now, before I decide how to deal with you, I suggest we all calm down and pay our respects to the Eye of Fire. We should never have lost faith and believed it could harm us!' Solemnly, Enzo beckoned for Luca and Bella to join him and they inserted the three keys

118

into the keyholes hidden among the intricately carved dancing elephants on the casket.

Emily, Jack and Scott grinned at each other, buzzing with excitement. They had solved Operation Ruby and saved the Eye of Fire from falling into the wrong hands. And now they were going to get a proper look at the fabulous gem.

Enzo Romaldi eased open the wooden lid.

Emily craned forward for a better view of the ruby.

But the casket was empty.

Fifteen

The Really Obvious Elephant

N̲o one said a word.

Enzo let the lid drop. Then he opened it again. The white satin cushion was still bare. Luca reached in and picked it up and shook it – as if the ruby might somehow have slipped beneath it. It hadn't.

Scott felt Emily grasp his arm so hard she was in danger of amputating it at the elbow with her fingernails. He heard Jack mumble, *No way!* under his breath.

Suddenly, Tony Romaldi threw back his head and roared with laughter. But it wasn't the manic cackle of a criminal mastermind whose evil plot has come to fruition, Scott thought, more the over-the-top guffaw of a comedian laughing at his own unfunny joke.

'Don't look at me!' Tony laughed. 'I wouldn't have gone to all this trouble,' he waved his hand at Anna, still slumped on the sofa in her red sari, 'if I could've just helped myself to the ruby. I don't have a key, remember, since Dad gave it to Luca here!'

'Well, who *did* take it then?' Barbara shouted, putting into words the question that was hanging in the air like the smell of yesterday's fish pie in the school canteen. 'It takes all three keys to open that casket.'

'Well,' Tony sneered, 'why don't you ask my darling little brother?'

Grumbles of surprise and disagreement broke out round the caravan.

'Everyone worships good old *Luca*, don't they?' Tony pretended to bow down to his younger brother. 'But think about it! Who has a key? *Luca!* And who has access to his little daughter's key?' He looked at Bella – who glared back at him with her dark eyes flashing. 'Let me think!' Tony went on. 'Oh, yes, that would be Luca, too. He only has to wait for Dad to fall asleep over his after-dinner brandy and "borrow" his key and he's got the full set!'

'Yeah, the full set!' Danny parroted, holding up three fingers in case anyone had missed the point.

'How dare you?' Enzo seethed.

'That's *crazy*!' Luca yelled. 'Why would *I* want to steal the ruby?'

Tony shrugged. 'You tell me!' And, with that, he stormed out of the caravan slamming the door behind him.

Danny followed his father towards the door. Scott stopped him and held out his hand. Reluctantly, Danny handed over Scott's mobile phone. Scott had noticed it sticking out of Danny's pocket. He must have pinched it during their brawl.

Anna Romaldi slunk out after her son and husband. Jack held up the wig and veils. 'Don't forget these!' he called after her.

She didn't reply.

—

'Wow! *Amazing!*' Bella gazed through the porthole window in Emily's bedroom on the eighth floor. It was the morning after the vanishing ruby incident, and the friends had arranged to meet at The Lighthouse. They'd invited Bella along too, hoping to cheer her up. So far it seemed to be working. 'You're so lucky to live in a *real lighthouse*,' she told Emily. 'You can see everything from up here. There's the circus on the common – the big top, the lorries, even our caravan.' Bella lowered the binoculars and sighed. 'I bet Mum and Dad are in there now, arguing again. Mum keeps telling Dad not to worry, but he's really depressed about the ruby being missing.'

'I'm not surprised,' Scott said. 'It *was* a bit of a bombshell!'

Bella sighed again. 'The worst part of it is that people are actually starting to take that stupid rumour Uncle Tony started seriously. This morning everyone was talking about how Dad's the only one who could have got hold of all three keys.' She sank down on a beanbag. 'I wish I had a *normal* family like you guys.'

'Yeah, right!' Jack wasn't sure that his and Scott's family scored that highly on the Normal Scale either. Their dad was great – as dads go – but he was always off digging up ancient pots on the other side of the world. And Jack couldn't remember his mum, who'd died in a car crash when he was a baby. Emily's parents were cool, but a retired rock guitarist and a crazy Spanish artist who ran a Bed and Breakfast in an old lighthouse didn't *exactly* tick all the Normality Boxes either. *Although Em's mum does make very good chocolate brownies*, he thought, helping himself to a third.

Bella sniffed back a tear. 'There's no way Dad would have done something like that!' Suddenly her face brightened. 'Hey, do you think we could try and find out who *did* steal the Eye of Fire and prove Dad's innocent?'

'Try stopping us!' Jack laughed.

Emily was sitting on her bed with Drift on her lap. She looked up from her notebook and smiled at Bella. She'd already written *OPERATION RUBY (Phase Two)* at the top of a new page. 'First, we need a brainstorming session to draw up our list of suspects. As always, it comes down to Motive and Opportunity. Who wanted to steal the ruby, and who had the chance to do it?'

'Well, we *know* Tony, Danny and Anna had a motive,' Scott reasoned. 'But we can rule them out. Like Tony said, they wouldn't have needed to dream up that whole Syamantaka scheme if they could just nick the ruby instead.'

Emily chewed her pen. 'Hmm. Could it be a double bluff, though? I think we should keep them on the list for now.'

'But they've gone,' Bella said. 'They packed up and left this morning.'

'Does *anyone* else have a key to the casket apart from you, your dad and your grandfather?' Scott asked Bella.

Bella shook her head.

Scott raked his fingers through his floppy fringe as he thought. 'Which means *either* someone picked the locks, *or* they got hold of the keys and made copies.'

'And it's got to be a member of the circus,' Jack said, through a mouthful of brownie, 'since we're the only "outsiders" who know about the ruby.'

By the time Bella had to leave an hour later, Emily's notebook contained a list of about twenty suspects – including most of the circus performers, technicians and other crew.

'We'll start interviewing suspects tomorrow,' Emily explained, as she saw Bella out of The Lighthouse.

Bella gave Emily a hug. 'Thank you! I'm so lucky to have friends like you and Scott and Jack. And Drift, of course,' she added, stooping to ruffle the little dog's fur.

Emily watched Bella run off along the promontory towards the village, her long plait swinging behind her. A sad sinking feeling pulled at her like an undercurrent, but she smiled when Bella turned to wave.

When she returned to her room the boys were fighting over the last brownie. Emily sat down on her bed and took up her notebook. She added another name to the top of the suspect list. 'OK, now we've got to talk about the elephant in the room,' she sighed.

'Elephant?' Jack looked around as if he expected to see a stray trunk or tusk poking out from under the bed. 'What elephant?'

Scott slapped his forehead. 'It's just a saying, dumbo! It means a-really-obvious-thing-that-everyone's-avoiding-talking-about!'

'So what is this really obvious elephant?' Jack asked grumpily. He hated it when Scott knew stuff he didn't.

'Luca Romaldi,' Emily sighed. 'I couldn't say it when Bella was here, but he *has* to be our Number One Suspect.'

'Luca's the elephant?' Jack snorted, spraying brownie crumbs over the carpet. 'No way! Luca's a good bloke!'

'That's not exactly a watertight defence, is it?' Scott scoffed. 'Excuse me, your honour, the defendant couldn't possibly have committed this crime because he is *A Good Bloke!*'

'I hope I'm wrong about this too,' Emily said. 'But we can't let our emotions get in the way of an investigation. Tony was right: Luca has a key and he could easily have got hold of Bella's and Enzo's . . .'

'But Bella *never takes* that charm bracelet off!' Jack protested. 'She even keeps it on when they're performing. She just puts tape over it . . .' Jack's voice tailed off and he closed his eyes, trying to block out an unwelcome memory that was trying to gatecrash his brain.

'What is it?' Emily demanded.

Now it was Jack's turn to sigh. 'Remember when we went to the lake? Luca insisted on Bella leaving her bracelet with him.'

Scott nodded slowly. 'Oh, yes, that's right. He said he didn't want her to lose it. He'd have had plenty of time to get a copy made while we were at Polhallow Lake. Then he'd only have needed Enzo's key. You have to admit, it doesn't look good for Luca.'

Jack wasn't giving up that easily. 'OK, so maybe Luca had the opportunity. That doesn't mean he did it! What's his motive, for a start?'

Emily snapped her notebook shut. 'You're right. But we *have* to look into it.'

'We can't expect Bella to investigate her own dad!' Scott pointed out.

Emily had already thought of that. 'We'll have to run Operation Ruby on two levels. You two run the *official* operation tomorrow, interviewing suspects at the circus with Bella. Meanwhile, Drift and I will *go dark*. We'll run a *covert* operation tailing Luca Romaldi and see what we can dig up. And let's hope we find something that eliminates him from our enquiries.' Emily held up both hands with her fingers crossed.

Sixteen

Sleight of Hand

'Emily will join us later,' Jack told Bella when she opened the door to her caravan the following afternoon, still wearing her tracksuit after the morning's rehearsals. 'She's gone to the dentist.'

'She's taken Drift to the . . .' Scott said at the same time.

Bella looked puzzled. 'Emily's taken Drift to the *dentist*?'

Now Jack wished he and Scott had talked through Emily's alibi earlier. 'Er, yeah,' he bluffed. 'It's this special dentist in Carrickstowe. They do human teeth *and* dog teeth. Cool, eh?'

Remind me, Scott thought, *if I ever commit a crime and need someone to cover for me, not to ask Jack.* 'Come on, let's go and interview Aidan McDonald first,' he said, hastily changing the subject. 'I just saw him sharpening his swords in the big top.'

Meanwhile, Emily was watching from behind a chestnut tree. She waited until the boys and Bella were safely in the big top and then crept over and peeped through a window at the back of the caravan. Luca was sitting at the kitchen table sorting through a pile of papers. He was making the same baffled face her dad did when he was looking through bank statements and bills – like someone trying to work out a really hard maths problem. *Money worries?* Emily asked herself. *The classic motive for theft.*

Emily's suspicions were strengthened when Sylvia Romaldi entered the caravan.

'I'm back!' she called, as she staggered into the kitchen with bags of food shopping. Luca quickly bundled the papers off the table into a drawer. He kept hold of one letter, folded it and stuffed it in his jeans pocket.

'Hi, love,' he said in an over-cheery voice. 'I've just got to pop out for a minute. I'll make you a cup of tea when I get back.'

Emily groaned under her breath. Whatever was in those papers, Luca hadn't told his wife about it. *Secret* money worries. This was going from bad to worse. Had Luca stolen the ruby to pay off his debts? 'Don't jump to conclusions!' Emily muttered to Drift. 'Maybe he hid the papers because he's organizing a surprise holiday for Sylvia or something.' She wished she could believe it. For once, she really didn't want to be right.

When Luca left the caravan a few moments later, Emily and Drift followed at a safe distance. She felt bad about deceiving Bella and snooping on Luca like this, and had to remind herself it was for the best. But she'd been *hoping* to uncover something that would clear Luca's name and prove he *wasn't* the thief. So far, things weren't going to plan.

Luca Romaldi didn't go far. He walked across the grass to the parking area and slipped round the back of one of the large trucks. When he didn't reappear after a few minutes, Emily and Drift crept along the side of the next parked truck and peeped round the end.

Luca was leaning against the bumper of the truck speaking into his mobile phone. 'I understand,' he was saying. 'But if you could just give me a little more time . . .' He looked down at the letter in his hand. 'I won't be late with the repayments in future. It's just that we've had a few family issues lately . . .' Luca glanced over his shoulder as if sensing he was being overheard. Emily ducked behind the truck. She strained to catch the rest of the conversation: *pay back the loan . . . as soon as possible . . . I promise . . .*

Emily had heard enough. She called Drift and trudged back towards the big top. In spite of the blue sky and sunshine she felt as if her own personal black cloud was hovering over her head. Luca Romaldi had secretly taken out a loan and he was struggling to repay it. This didn't look good at all. But how was she ever going to tell Bella? It would break her friend's heart. Suddenly she heard her name and looked up to see Bella skipping towards her over the daisies, followed by Jack and Scott.

'Hey, Emily!' Bella called. 'Are your teeth OK? And Drift's?'

'Er, fine thanks. How are yours?' Emily replied, feeling very confused. Was this some traditional circus greeting, like actors saying *break a leg?*

'No fillings or anything *at the dentist?*' Scott asked pointedly.

Emily finally cottoned on: the dentist was her cover story. 'Yeah, teeth all good, thanks! So, how did you get on with the Sword of Persia?'

Scott shrugged as they walked towards the caravans. 'I don't think Aidan McDonald knows anything about the ruby going missing. Bit of a waste of time.'

'How can you say that?' Jack laughed. 'He let me have a go on his bed of nails. Awesome!'

'So, which suspect shall we interview next?' Bella asked eagerly.

Emily didn't know what to say. Luckily Scott came to the rescue.

'What about Mike Turnbull?' he suggested. 'Look, he's over by his caravan doing magic tricks for a bunch of little kids again.'

'Oh, yeah, the old pulling-the-watch-out-of-the-earhole routine,' Jack said. 'Good idea. I wanted to ask him how he does those tricks anyway.'

'He's hardly going to tell you all his trade secrets, is he?' Scott laughed.

The friends waited for the gang of kids to drift away, then strolled over.

'Those sleight of hand tricks are awesome,' Jack told Mike. 'Where did you learn that stuff?'

Mike smiled. 'I was a street magician for years but there's not much money in it and the psychic act works better as a stage show. You have to be up close to do things like this.' He held out his hand and unfurled his fingers. In his palm was a fine gold chain.

'That's mine!' Emily cried, her hand flying to her neck. 'I can't believe it!'

Mike winked at the boys with his green eye, while looking at Emily and Bella with the black one. Then he opened his other hand. It held a small metal disk.

Emily looked closer. 'That's Drift's name tag from his collar!' Drift, meanwhile, was busy watching Mimi being groomed outside the next-door caravan. 'Drift, I'm ashamed of you!' Emily scolded. But she couldn't be *too* hard on him. After all, she hadn't felt Mike take her necklace – and she prided herself on her powers of observation.

Emily looked at her friends and laughed. But underneath the laughter, her brain was running like a manic hamster in a wheel. Was there a teeny-tiny chance that Luca hadn't stolen the ruby, after all?

I hope Mike Turnbull can't really read minds, she thought, *because if he knew what I'm thinking right now, he wouldn't like it one little bit!*

Seventeen

The Spider Scheme

A few minutes later, the friends were settling down for a planning meeting in the tree house in the back garden at Stone Cottage. It had been the HQ for their last investigation, Operation Copycat, and was still a favourite meeting place. Bella was thrilled with it – especially the rope and basket for hoisting Drift up too. She made herself comfortable on the cushions with Scott and Emily, while Jack climbed into the hammock hanging between two branches above the platform.

Emily took out her notebook. She would have to write up her report on Luca Romaldi's money problems later when Bella wasn't around. Instead, she found Mike Turnbull's name on the suspect list, circled it and added two big stars for good measure. Then she asked the question that had been on her mind ever since she'd seen her necklace lying in the palm of Mike Turnbull's hand. 'Bella, could Mike have taken your bracelet with the key on it?'

Bella ran her fingers over her charm bracelet. 'During a show we're all crowded together in the wings. I guess he could have taken it before I taped it up. But only for a moment. I'd soon notice it was gone.'

Scott nodded. 'I was wondering the same thing. But to open the casket Mike would need to have had Enzo's key from his neck and Luca's from his watch at the same time. And Bella's right: people would realize their things were missing pretty quickly.'

'He'd only need each key for a moment so that he could make an impression of it,' Emily pointed out. 'Then he could get copies made from the impressions and use them to open the casket.'

'You can press the key into a bar of soap to make the impression,' Bella said. 'I saw that in a film where they were escaping from prison.'

Emily nodded. 'That's right. You just need something soft to make the casting mould – like wax or clay or soap. Then you melt some metal and pour it in. When it sets you have a replica key. You can even buy special little kits on-line.'

Scott raised his eyebrows. 'What websites have *you* been looking at, Em? *BurglaryMadeSimple.com*?'

Emily batted him with a cushion. 'I was looking at supplies for private investigators actually. I was just *browsing*.' Then she made another note in her book. 'Right, we need a plan of action. If Mike's stolen the ruby, he must have hidden it somewhere.'

Emily, Scott and Bella were trying to come up with a way of getting in to Mike Turnbull's caravan to search for the ruby, when they were disturbed by a shriek and a crash. They'd forgotten all about Jack dozing in his hammock. But now he was stamping around, slapping his legs and shaking his shorts as if doing some kind of extreme folk dance. 'Spider!' he yelled. 'Just crawled up my leg!'

Drift thought this was a new game and joined in with a move or two of his own.

'Was it a big one?' Bella asked, rushing to help.

'Massive!' Jack held up his hands to indicate something the size of a tarantula. 'I swear it had *fur*!'

Scott bugged his eyes into a horrified stare. 'Oh, no! That sounds like a Cornish tree spider! Their bite can be fatal.'

'*Fatal?*' Jack gulped. He was in a blind panic now, hyperventilating and trying to pull his shorts down.

Emily reached across and scooped up a small black spider from Jack's knee, if only to spare Bella the sight of Jack dancing around in his underpants. Jack took one look and wrestled Scott to the floor in revenge for the Cornish tree spider joke.

Bella laughed. 'It's funny. The only other person I've ever seen who's *that* scared of spiders is Mike Turnbull. He saw one in the big top the other day and I thought he was going to have a heart attack.'

Emily stared at her. 'Bella, that's brilliant!' She popped the spider into a matchbox she kept in her bag for collecting evidence. 'This little guy is our passport to Mike Turnbull's caravan!' Then she told them the plan.

It was lunchtime the following day before there was a chance to put the spider scheme into operation. Mike Turnbull was sitting in a deck chair outside his caravan eating a sandwich. The friends wandered over and struck up a conversation.

'Could you show me how to do that necklace-nicking trick?' Jack asked politely.

'Uggh!' Emily shrieked, 'Gross!' She stared at Turnbull, clapped her hand over her mouth and jumped up and down in terror. 'That's the biggest spider I've ever seen!' It was all an act, of course. Emily wasn't even the tiniest bit afraid of spiders.

At the same moment, Scott leaned over and quickly let the 'Cornish tree spider' slip out of the matchbox onto Mike Turnbull's chair.

'Agggghh!' Mike shrieked as the spider crawled up his leg. He leaped out of his chair, nearly choking on his sandwich.

Jack also did a vertical take-off at the sight of his old eight-legged enemy, adding to the general chaos.

'It's OK. I've got it.' Scott scooped the spider up. He popped it carefully back in the box hidden in his pocket but at the last moment pretended to drop it. 'Oh, no, it's got away!'

'Where's it gone now?' Mike stammered, his pale face whiter than ever.

Emily pointed at the open door. 'It just crawled into your caravan.'

Mike stared at the door. He looked as if he might faint.

'Don't worry, we'll get rid of it for you,' Scott offered.

'Would you?' Mike Turnbull collapsed into his deck chair. 'Thank you so much.'

Like speeding bullets, the four friends shot into the caravan. They shouted spider-hunting phrases to each other – *It's crawled under the rug!* and *Quick, there it goes!* – all the while searching everywhere for something far more valuable and much less, well, *spidery*. Mike Turnbull's caravan was small and it was spotlessly clean and tidy. It was soon obvious there was no sign of the missing ruby.

'Have you found it yet?' Mike asked in a quavering voice, popping his head round the door.

Scott leaped across the room and pounced on an armchair. 'Gotcha!' He held up his cupped hands. Emily passed him the matchbox and he pretended to stuff the spider inside. 'Would you like to see it?' Scott asked innocently, waving the box under Mike's nose and starting to slide it open.

'No, take it away!' Mike squeaked, his eyes wide with fear. But once the dreaded beast had been released into the wild, he recovered his composure and handed around ice creams by way of thanks.

Emily might have felt quite guilty about playing the spider trick on Mike Turnbull if it hadn't been for one thing. They may not have found any stolen rubies stashed away in the caravan, but she *had* found a little box containing small ingots of metal and some modelling clay tucked neatly into his desk drawer.

Jack, Scott and Bella could hardly contain their excitement when they got back to the tree house and Emily showed them the photo she'd snapped on her phone.

'That modelling clay would make a perfect mould,' Emily explained. 'And the metal could be used to cast the key. It's probably something with a low melting point like tin or lead.'

Jack grinned. Sometimes it was worrying, the stuff Emily knew! Then he high-fived with Bella. 'Old Freaky-Eyes is our jewel thief.'

'And this proves Dad didn't do it,' Bella sighed happily. 'I can't wait to tell everyone.'

'Hang on,' Scott said. 'We can't be sure he was using this stuff for copying the keys to the casket. He might just be into making model toy soldiers or something.'

'Er, did you *see* any toy soldiers in his caravan?' Jack scoffed.

'Scott's right,' Emily agreed reluctantly. 'It's possible these materials are for something perfectly innocent. We need more evidence.'

Jack sighed with impatience. Why did Emily always have to agree with Scott when he was being *boring*? 'So what do you suggest? That we just ask Mike Turnbull if he'd mind showing us where he's hidden the ruby?'

Emily's face lit up. 'Jack, you're a genius!' she exclaimed. 'But we won't *ask* him to show us the hiding place. We'll *trick* him into it!'

Jack groaned. 'Please tell me this isn't going to involve spiders again.'

'No spiders I promise,' Emily laughed. 'We just have to arrange for Bella to rush into a room when Mike Turnbull's there, and pretend to be all excited because someone has found the ruby. From that moment on, we keep Mike under constant surveillance. If we're right, sooner or later he'll sneak off and check his hiding place to see whether it's *really* been discovered – and we'll be right behind him.'

'Awesome plan,' Jack breathed. 'Yep, you were right, Em. I *am* a genius.'

'Do you think you can do it, Bella?' Scott asked. 'You'll have to put on a good act.'

Bella nodded seriously. 'Of course I can if there's a chance this will prove Dad's innocent. And I know the perfect time to do it: just before the start of the show tonight. Mike and a few of the others always sit at the back of the big top and play poker while the technicians run through the light- and soundchecks.'

'If Mike Turnbull moves a muscle,' Jack said, 'we'll catch him.'

Eighteen

Eyeball to Eyeball

The plan worked perfectly!

'Has anyone seen my mum?' Bella shouted, flying into the big top. 'I've got to tell her. The Eye of Fire has reappeared! It's back in the casket!'

Ray, the comedic acrobat, Aidan McDonald and Mike Turnbull were playing poker, using an upturned crate as a table. Ray looked up from his cards and smiled. 'Hey, that's great news, Bella! Last time I saw your mum she was in the wings repairing a headdress.'

'Thanks,' Bella called over her shoulder as she ran off.

Outside the big top, Scott couldn't help admiring Bella's acting abilities. It was a big gamble for her. If their plan backfired, she could end up in major trouble for pretending the ruby had been found.

Scott watched Mike Turnbull. He'd already applied his stage make-up ready for his Incognito act, which meant he was pea-green from the waist up. He was studying his cards intently and had barely blinked since Bella's announcement. *Is he just concentrating on the game,* Scott wondered, *or is he trying to look unruffled by Bella's announcement, while secretly planning to go and check his hiding place?*

Slowly, Mike laid down his cards. 'Royal Flush,' he said with a smile.

The other players groaned and threw in their cards.

'That'll teach us to play poker with a mind-reader!' Aidan McDonald laughed. He was also in full stage costume. The leather and metal body armour of the Sword of Persia creaked and jangled as he moved.

Mike Turnbull checked his watch. 'Count me out of the next hand, guys. I just remembered I want to set the TV to record a programme tonight.' He got up and strolled towards the exit.

Scott felt excitement pulse down his spine as he exchanged double thumbs-up signs with Jack and Emily.

Jack grinned and turned to follow Mike.

'We can't *all* tail him,' Emily whispered. 'He'll see us. I'll go with Drift.' She took her phone from her shoulder bag and stuffed it in her shorts pocket, then handed the bag to Jack. 'Hang on to this. I'll call you as soon as I see what he's up to.'

Before the boys could object, Emily had slipped away, edging around the big top as silently as a lioness stalking her prey.

Jack stuck his hands in his pockets. 'Yeah, right, you go on your own,' he muttered sulkily. 'We'll just stand here like lemons, shall we?' He looked down at Emily's shoulder bag. 'Lemons with handbags!'

'She does have a point,' Scott said. 'You're about as stealthy as a herd of rhinos auditioning for *Stomp!* Let's go and find Bella and wait for Em to call us.'

⸺

Meanwhile, Emily spotted Mike Turnbull emerging from the main entrance of the big top. To her surprise, he didn't head towards the caravans, but hurried round to the far side of the big top, ducking under the guy ropes as he went. He didn't stop until he came to one of the huge storage lorries. Emily knew from Bella that this was where most of the bulky props and equipment for the show were stored overnight. They were carried in and out of the wings on trolleys when they were needed for the various acts.

Turnbull glanced over his shoulder. Emily and Drift melted into the shadows. He unlocked the back of the truck and pulled open the double doors with a metallic clang. Then he folded down a set of steps, climbed up and disappeared inside.

Emily tiptoed across the grass with Drift at her heels, pressed herself flat against the side of the truck and, hardly daring to breathe, peeped round the edge of the door. She shrank back with a start, her heart rattling against her rib-cage. Mike Turnbull was kneeling just inside the truck, opening the fabulous golden treasure chest that was used as a prop in the Aladdin's Cave scene in the show. Emily knew it was full of jewels – very big, very sparkly, very *plastic* jewels – that spilled out all over the circus ring. *Of course*, Emily thought. *Where better to hide a* real *ruby than in a great big box of artificial gems? I'll just take one last little peek to be sure*, she decided, *and then I'll head back to tell the others.*

That last peek turned out to be the worst decision Emily had made for a very long time. She found herself eyeball to eyeball with Mike Turnbull. One green eye. One black eye. Both burning with menace. Emily grabbed Drift and turned to run. But it was too late. Mike Turnbull clapped one hand over her mouth, wrapped the other arm round her shoulders and bundled her into the back of the lorry. Emily glimpsed a blur of fur as Drift jumped behind the treasure chest. Then she heard the doors slamming shut.

Emily fell against a mountain of rolled-up rugs. *If only one of these was a magic carpet that could get me out of this.* But there was no escape. Turnbull pinned her arms to her sides and began tying her hands behind her back with nylon cord.

'So you thought you could follow me, did you?' he spat. 'Hard luck! The whole trick of a mind-reading act is being able to pick up the tiniest little signals: body language, tone of voice. I *thought* Bella was lying about the ruby, but I couldn't be sure. And then I heard your little footsteps behind me. You're good, I'll give you that. Quieter than most. Just not quite good *enough.*'

Emily thrashed and kicked but Turnbull was too strong. He held her legs down and bound her ankles while he continued to talk. 'And then I put two and two together. I realized you kids duped me with that spider routine this morning too. Nosing round my caravan, weren't you? I'd have seen through your play-acting that time as well if I hadn't been so flustered. I just can't think straight when there are spiders around. I don't know how you knew that but it was a stroke of genius. I have to admire you.'

'Well, stop tying me up if you admire me so much!' Emily snapped as the rope bit into her skin.

Turnbull shrugged. 'Sorry. It's too late for that.'

'We know you stole the ruby,' Emily told him, 'so you might as well let me go. My friends will be here looking for me in a minute.'

'What a shame I won't be sticking around for a chat,' Turnbull said with a sneer. His face was so green it was like talking to a mutant cabbage. 'I was going to wait a couple of weeks before leaving so as not to arouse suspicion, but now you little snoopers have discovered my retirement plan I'll have to get out of here straight away. And I'll be taking this with me.' He pulled a large red gem from his pocket. The Eye of Fire glowed in the light from a tiny window high in the wall of the lorry.

'But why?' Emily asked, staring at the magnificent ruby in Turnbull's hand.

'Why do you *think*? It's worth a fortune! I'm sick of grafting away every night for next to nothing. When I heard the Romaldis were planning to hand the ruby over to the Indian authorities anyway, I thought, why not? It'll just be sitting in a museum or something.'

'So you used your sleight of hand skills to get hold of the three keys?' Emily prompted. 'And then you made copies of them?'

'You *have* been doing your homework, haven't you?' Turnbull slid the ruby back into his pocket. 'Now, I'm sorry about this, but I want you out of the way for a while until I can get out of here.'

And with those words, Mike Turnbull tied a scarf over Emily's mouth, lifted her up and dropped her inside an enormous terracotta Ali Baba jar. Then he screwed the lid on.

Inside the pot Emily leaned against the rough clay wall.

She could hear Turnbull moving around, then the doors of the lorry opening and closing as he left.

Emily tried to rock the pot to tip it over, but it was too heavy. She tried to wriggle her hands free of the ropes, but they were too tight. Turnbull clearly knew how to tie a good knot. *Mmmph* she cried, biting on the thick folds of the gag. She slumped down and tried to hold back tears of frustration. It was hot inside the pot, and dark. All except for a row of funny little slits down each side, which let in rays of light. The light criss-crossed her body like *Star Wars* lightsabers.

That's when Emily realized where she was.

This wasn't just any pot. This was the Ali Baba jar that the Sword of Persia used in his act. And if she didn't get out soon it wouldn't be lightsabers coming in through those holes.

It would be razor-sharp swords!

Nineteen

Drift the Stunt-Dog

Drift scratched at the pot with his paws. He knew Emily was in there, but what was she doing? Was it a game of hide and seek? No, Emily wouldn't have hidden without him. Now Drift wished he'd barked at that strange green man, or bitten him, or something. Why had he put Emily into this big pot? It made no sense. Then again, humans did a lot of things that made no sense, like wearing clothes and eating cucumber.

It was all so confusing. But there was one thing Drift *did* know: Emily was afraid. He could *smell* her fear through those little holes in the pot. He scratched again to tell her he was there.

Drift couldn't bear Emily being scared. He backed into a corner and shivered. He tucked his tail and ears down. Maybe she was stuck in there. Drift had been stuck down a rabbit hole once. He'd still be down there if Emily hadn't pulled him out. And now he knew Emily needed his help. There was another *mmmppph* from the pot. It sounded like the noise Jack and Scott made when they were cushion-fighting. *That's it. Brainwave!* Jack and Scott would know what to do.

Must. Find. Boys. Drift sniffed every millimetre of the walls of the lorry for a way out. But the only whiff of fresh air was from a tiny window high up in the wall – higher even than a human could reach. He scrambled up onto a pile of carpets. But it was still too far to jump. And you'd have to be a squirrel to climb up there. Or a cat. Drift hated to admit it, but climbing was one thing that cats *were* good for. The only *dog* he knew who could climb was Mimi.

Drift's ears perked up at the thought of Mimi. *Mimi* could do one of her awesome balancing acts to get to that window. But Mimi wasn't there. In frustration, Drift butted his nose against a long pole propped up against the wall next to the carpets. He leaped back, startled, as it toppled over.

152

Drift stared at the pole. It had fallen at an angle against the back wall. The end had lodged in the corner of the little window. If he were Mimi, or – horrible thought – if he were a *cat*, he could run along that pole and reach the window. He gave the pole an experimental prod with his paw. It wobbled.

Mmmph! The noise came from inside the pot again.

Drift knew he couldn't let Emily down. He braced his tail and put one paw on the pole and then another. His paw slipped and he fell. He growled and started again. He remembered how Mimi did it – looking straight ahead, tail up, back straight – and he tried to copy her. That worked better. He pictured Mimi's little pink pom-pom tail bobbing along ahead of him. That worked even better.

Inside the pot, Emily had heard Drift scrabble on the pot. Then she heard a loud clang followed by more scrabbling, some growling and several thuds. What was Drift *doing*? Skateboarding round the lorry by the sound of it. Or break-dancing! If only she could tell him to go and fetch the boys. *Mmmph!*

On the seventh attempt Drift made it to the top of the pole. He felt very pleased with himself, but resisted the temptation to do a little victory dance.

There was a wire mesh over the window but the pole had knocked it loose. Drift grabbed the corner with his teeth and shook it like a rat. *Grrr!* He fell off the pole. But at least the mesh tore away and fell with him. Now all he had to do was climb that pole one more time and jump through the window. He climbed, he jumped, he scrabbled his way to the window. He yelped with pain as two of his claws ripped off on the sharp metal edge. But at last he was through.

Then there was the problem of getting down the other side.

He didn't have a concept of *gravity*, of course, but it formed the key element of his plan. OK, the *only* element of his plan.

Emily wondered why it had suddenly gone so quiet. Had Drift fallen asleep? Or had he hurt himself with all that crashing about? Suddenly, she heard the lorry doors opening. *Thank goodness!* The boys must have worked out she was in here. *Mmmpph!* It was the only sound she could make through the gag. Why weren't they opening the jar?

There was a jolt and a judder. Emily fell against the side as the jar tipped and moved at an angle. She could hear wheels beneath her. *We must be going down a ramp on a trolley*. She could tell by the light that they were outside now, wheeling across the grass. *Mmmpph!* she cried, trying to alert the trolley-pusher, but he was singing an Elvis Presley number at the top of his voice and didn't hear her. They were inside again now, rolling over a smooth surface. Emily could hear applause and cheering. Then there was silence. *Where am I?*

Then she heard a voice ring out. '. . . and now the Sword

of Persia, a man who laughs in the face of peril . . .' It was Enzo Romaldi. She was in the circus ring and the show had started.

Emily had seen the act twice. She pictured the Sword of Persia setting swords alight and swallowing them. Now he was juggling with knives and throwing them at the target while Mariannne danced in front of it. Now he was swishing more swords about and slicing watermelons in half to show how sharp they were.

She knew exactly what was coming next.

Frantic with terror, Emily tried to pull her hands free, bang her head on the side of the pot, or scream, or shout . . . She remembered how she'd wished she could see inside the pot and work out the trick to getting out. But even if she *knew* the trick, it wouldn't help. She was so tightly bound she was powerless to do *anything*.

And now she could hear the terrible words. 'I will insert six swords through this empty jar,' the Sword of Persia proclaimed. 'You will see that they go right through and come out the other side.'

This was the end. Emily wished it would hurry up and be over. Waiting for the cold touch of the blades was torture.

She thought of her mum and her dad. She thought of Drift.

'And now, in goes the first sword . . .'

Twenty

Stop the Show!

'What's taking Emily so long?' Jack grumbled as he hung around outside the big top with Scott and Bella. 'I'm fed up of lugging her handbag around. It doesn't suit me for a start.'

'I hope she's OK,' Bella said, winding her plait up on top of her head. She'd changed into her red sequined outfit ready for the show, which would be starting any minute. The Flying Romaldis would be going ahead with a reduced version of their trapeze act, even though Tony and Danny were missing. Crowds had been pouring into the big top and the air was thick with the smell of hotdogs and candy-floss.

Scott was worried too. They'd looked everywhere and he'd tried calling Emily's phone. But she – and Mike Turnbull – had disappeared.

'Look, there's Drift!' Jack cried.

The little dog was hurtling towards them across the grass as if powered by rocket fuel. Scott grinned at Bella and Jack in relief. Emily couldn't be far away. But as Drift drew closer, Scott's worries came flooding back. The little dog was limping and there was blood on his front paws.

Scott, Jack and Bella all stroked Drift's fur and cuddled him. He was panting heavily, his long pink tongue lolling from his jaws. He was clearly exhausted, but managed to lick them all in greeting.

'Where's Emily?' Scott asked.

Drift pricked up his ears and trotted away, heading for the back of the big top.

'He's taking us to her,' Jack cried. 'Come on!'

Drift made for the back of a lorry and stood on his hind legs with his front paws on the bumper.

'What's in there?' Scott asked Bella.

'Just some of the big equipment for the show.' Bella punched numbers into the combination lock, and between them they pulled open the doors and climbed inside the lorry. It looked to Scott like a cross between a junk shop and the school P. E. cupboard, a jumble of carpets and crash mats and platforms and ladders and lanterns.

'Em, it's us!' Scott called. 'Where are you?'

His voice bounced off the metal walls of the lorry. Jack waded through a mound of fake jewels to look in a huge treasure chest. 'She's not here. What's the deal, Drift?'

Drift was scratching at a patch on the floor. He kept looking up with his head on one side and his ears trembling.

Scott knelt and examined the spot. There was a ring in the grease as if something had been standing there. 'What do you think could have made this mark?' he asked Bella.

Bella looked around to see what was missing. 'It must be the Ali Baba pot.' She glanced at Jack's watch. 'They'll have taken it into the ring by now. Aidan will just be starting his act.'

'You mean that big jar that the Sword of Persia sticks his swords through?' Jack asked.

Suddenly an appalling thought crashed into Scott's head like a speeding car skidding out of control. 'You don't think Emily could be *in* that pot, do you?' he mumbled.

'No way!' Jack laughed. 'Not unless she's got a death wish.'

Scott shook his head. 'I'm not saying she climbed inside just for the fun of it. What if Turnbull tied her up and shut her in there?'

Jack's laughter died in his mouth. He stared at Drift still padding round in circles and realized Scott could be right. But then he thought of something. 'She'll be OK though. Aidan looks inside first to show the audience the pot's empty. He'll see Emily's in there.'

But Bella shook her head. Her face had turned a ghostly white. 'No, he doesn't. He slides all the swords in first. *Then* he shows the audience the inside of the pot so they can see how the swords have gone all the way through. If Emily's in there . . .' Bella couldn't finish the sentence. She shuddered. 'We've got to *do* something!'

Scott took hold of Bella's elbows to steady her. 'OK, quick. Tell me. What's the way out of the pot? How does Marianne avoid being stabbed when she's in there?'

'The pot is placed over a trapdoor,' Bella explained urgently. 'She flips open the bottom of the pot and slides the trapdoor to one side. Then she drops through into the space under the ring and waits until all the swords are out again before coming back up.'

'But Emily won't be able to do that if she's tied up,' Jack groaned.

'Here's what we do,' Scott said, already on his way out of the lorry. 'You two go and get Aidan to stop the act. I'll crawl in under the staging and open that trapdoor in case you don't make it in time.'

'All the trapdoors have labels painted on them,' Bella said, hurrying down the ladder. 'The one you want is marked QR-3. It stands for Quick Release Three.'

'Take this!' Jack thrust the torch out of Emily's bag at Scott. Then – with Drift sprinting ahead of them – he and Bella ran faster than they'd ever run before.

Jack, Bella and Drift barrelled into the big top and hurtled down the nearest aisle, tripping over bags and feet and causing mayhem as they went. Jack took no notice. All he cared about was reaching the ring and stopping the show. He could see the Sword of Persia and Marianne, in her belly-dancer costume, standing either side of the Ali Baba jar.

'Stop!' Jack yelled, throwing himself into the ring. 'There's someone in the pot!'

The Sword of Persia looked up. To Jack's horror, he now saw that two swords had already been inserted through the jar. He thought he was going to be sick. *It was too late.*

Drift ran to the pot. He scratched at the side and barked.

'It's true!' Bella screamed. 'Emily's in there.'

Marianne clapped her hand over her mouth and staggered backwards.

There was a buzz of excitement from the audience.

They thought this was all part of the act.

Aidan McDonald stared at Jack and Bella. For a moment he looked angry, then horrified as he realized they were serious.

Very slowly, he unscrewed the lid of the pot and looked inside.

Twenty-one

An Unexpected Twist

Meanwhile, Scott was shining the torch at the underside of the circus ring, desperately searching for a trapdoor marked QR-3. Every muscle in his body was burning with pain as he crawled around like a deranged caterpillar. If Incognito could read Scott's mind right now, he'd find that his deepest wish wasn't fame or fortune, or even to play right-back for Chelsea;

it was simply to rescue Emily. And then stand up and stretch his legs.

He collapsed and lay face down, his nose pressed to the grass. If only he could rest for a few minutes. But he couldn't give up. Emily's life was at stake. He spurred himself on to the next trapdoor and shone the torch at the white painted letters. *QR-3.* This was it! Trembling with exhaustion, Scott slid the trapdoor to one side. There was some kind of clay surface in the way. *Of course, the base of the pot.* How was he going to open it from underneath? He jabbed at it with the heel of his hand in frustration. To his surprise, it sprang open.

⸺

Just a few feet above Scott's head, Jack watched the Sword of Persia look down into the Ali Baba jar. Time stood still. Jack was no longer aware of the lights or the music or the murmurs from the audience. He barely registered Bella gripping his hand. His whole world zoomed in to Aidan McDonald's face, as if he were looking down the wrong end of a telescope.

At long last, Aidan looked up. He flourished his sword above his head and smiled. 'Ladies and gentlemen, please do not be alarmed.' He tipped the jar over and rolled it from one side of the ring to the other to show everyone what was inside.

Jack couldn't believe it.

The jar was empty!

Suddenly Marianne snapped back from her near fainting-fit. She did a few belly-dancing moves, and addressed the audience. 'Please say hello to the youngest member of the Romaldi Circus, Miss Bella Romaldi. You'll see her later on the flying trapeze.' There was a round of applause, while Bella – a true professional – smiled and waved and executed a perfect set of backflips.

Jack almost collapsed with relief. It was OK! Emily hadn't been cut to shreds by razor-sharp swords. Then he looked up and realized the entire audience was staring at him. He shuffled towards the back of the ring wishing one of the trapdoors would open up and swallow him. He'd never felt so embarrassed. Or so confused. Emily hadn't been skewered in the pot, but she *had* disappeared off the face of the planet. Drift looked just as puzzled. He was running round in circles searching for her everywhere.

'Perhaps *you'd* like to go in the Ali Baba jar, Bella?' The Sword of Persia asked, smiling and making the best of the unexpected twist to his act. Bella gave a thumbs-up. He lifted her in and replaced the lid.

Bella wasn't afraid, of course. She knew exactly how to work the trick. But her mind was in a spin. What had happened to Emily? Had Scott got to the trapdoor first and let her out? Or was she still in danger somewhere else? But there was no time to think about that now. She opened the base of the pot and then the trapdoor and tapped three times on the inside of the jar to give the all-clear signal, before dropping down under the floor.

Bella lay on the grass and listened to the swords sliding through the jar above. She counted six blades going in, then began counting them out again. Suddenly she heard a commotion behind her.

'Scott?' she called out. 'Is that you?'

'Bella?' Scott's voice came back. 'I've got Emily. She's OK!'

Her heart skipping with relief, Bella heard the final sword slide out of the jar. 'See you up top,' she called, before climbing back up into the jar. 'Sorry about that,' she whispered to Aidan and Marianne as she jumped out of the pot again, smiling for the audience.

Then Bella ran to find Jack and Drift and tell them the good news.

＿

Scott felt as if he was stuck in an army assault course designed by a particularly fiendish sergeant major. When the base of the pot opened, Emily had fallen through the hole and landed in a wriggling heap on top of his head with a loud *Mmmppph!* He pulled the scarf from her mouth and cut the ropes from her wrists and ankles with his penknife. Together they began to commando crawl back to the hole at the edge of the circus ring – where

166

they could see a patch of light flooding in from outside. Emily's legs had gone to sleep after being squashed up inside the jar for so long, so she could only drag herself along like a beached mermaid. It seemed to take forever.

At last they made it to the side and Scott started to push Emily through the small gap in the wooden staging. She got half way through, but then found herself stuck fast, unable to propel the rest of her body with her legs. Just when Scott thought they'd be stuck there until the end of time, she was suddenly yanked through from the other side like a cork from a bottle.

Scott followed to find Emily lying on the grass gasping for air, while Jack and Bella hugged her and Drift licked her face. They fell on Scott with hugs (Bella) and high-fives (Jack) and licks (Drift).

'Awesome!' Jack laughed. 'You had us worried there, Em! We thought you'd have been sliced up like one of those watermelons by now.'

'Me too.' Emily's mouth was so dry from being gagged that the words came out as a feeble croak. Her wrists were red and sore where the ropes had dug into her skin and she still couldn't move her legs. But she didn't care. It was wonderful to be alive! She could still hardly believe it. The first sword had actually slid through the pot, missing her chest by millimetres as she shrank back against the side. She'd *seen* the tip of the second sword coming in from another angle and she'd known there was no way she could avoid that one too as it was aiming straight for her heart. It had been just touching her t-shirt when the bottom of the pot had opened and she'd fallen onto Scott's head. *If he'd been one second later . . .* Emily shuddered. She didn't want to think about it. She cuddled Drift to hide her tears of joy. Then she held him at arm's length. He was licking her nose so much she couldn't breathe.

'I still can't work out how Drift got out of the lorry,' Bella said.

Emily didn't know either. But he'd found a way and fetched help. He really was the best dog in the universe. And Jack, Scott and Bella were the best friends in the universe too.

'Just your basic *quick thinking and decisive action* eh, Drifty?' Jack laughed, ruffling his fur. 'He's been taking lessons from me.'

Scott rolled his eyes and punched Jack's arm. 'Taking lessons from Mimi, more like. He must have climbed that pole and jumped out through that little window.'

'Drift could join the circus any day!' Bella said proudly.

Drift wagged his tail. He felt very pleased with himself. Emily was out of that pot and laughing with her friends again. All was right with his world.

Suddenly Emily remembered how she'd landed up in the Ali Baba pot in the first place. 'We need to call the police.' Her voice still sounded as if she'd been gargling with gravel. 'We were right. Mike Turnbull has got the ruby.'

Bella sniffed back a tear. 'I *knew* it wasn't my dad.'

Emily put her arm round her.

'But why did he nick it?' Jack asked.

'For the money, of course.' Emily paused and felt in her pocket. 'Hang on. I'll let him tell you in his own words.'

Jack looked at Scott and Bella with a baffled shrug. Maybe Emily's near-death experience in the pot had sent her a bit, well . . . *potty*!

Emily grinned and held up her phone. 'I managed to press RECORD before he started tying me up. Listen!' She turned the volume to maximum and pressed PLAY. They listened in silence as Turnbull told Emily that he'd copied the keys and stolen the Eye of Fire.

'Cool! A full confession,' Scott whistled. 'Detective Inspector Hassan might as well go on holiday. We've done his job for him.'

'Bella! Come here now!'

The friends all looked up as Luca and Sylvia Romaldi shouted and waved from the big top.

Bella jumped up. 'Mum, Dad, I've got some amazing news.'

'It'll have to wait, love,' Luca said. 'We're on in a minute. You've got some flying to do, remember?'

Bella sped off towards her parents, flapping her out-stretched arms like wings. She was flying already.

Twenty-two

A Very Special Presentation

When the Romaldi Circus gave their final show in Castle Key the following Saturday, Emily, Scott, Jack and Drift were there, of course, in pride of place in the front row.

At the end of the show the audience clapped and cheered wildly as the performers all ran back into the ring to take their final bows. Gina hobbled into the ring on crutches too, her leg still in a plaster cast.

But just as people were starting to gather their things to leave, Enzo Romaldi jumped down from his white stallion – Moonlight was now fully recovered after the nail had been removed from his hoof – and took the microphone again. 'Tonight, it is my honour to make a very special presentation.'

The lights dimmed and a spotlight picked out the casket Enzo held in his hands, with its gold decorations and carved elephants. Enzo cleared his throat. 'On behalf of the Romaldi family, I am officially returning the Eye of Fire ruby to its rightful home.' He held up the casket and opened the lid to show the fabulous ruby, sparkling on its white satin cushion. The audience gasped in surprise. 'This ruby has been in the care of our family for two hundred years and has protected us from harm. But now it must return to India to the great Temple of Ganesha.'

A smartly dressed Indian man in a dark grey suit stepped forward. He looked a little out of place, as if he'd be more at home in a high-level business meeting than a circus, but he smiled and shook hands with Enzo. 'On behalf of the Board of Cultural Affairs, I thank the Romaldi family for their guardianship of the Eye of Fire ruby,' he said. 'And in recognition of your services to our nation, please accept this check for fifty thousand pounds.'

There was a round of applause and a dazzle of camera flashes as Enzo handed over the casket in return for a large white envelope.

Emily turned to Jack and Scott and smiled. Operation Ruby (Phase Two) had turned out perfectly. The police had caught Mike Turnbull trying to make his getaway. They'd stopped him for breaking the speed limit on the main road out of Carrickstowe towards London. Thanks to the evidence recorded on Emily's phone, he'd been arrested immediately and the ruby had been returned to Enzo Romaldi.

To Emily's great relief, it turned out that the secret debt she'd overheard Luca speaking about on the phone was simply a bank loan. He'd borrowed the money to invest in a much bigger big top for next season, so they could seat larger audiences and sell more tickets. It would allow them to make more money in the future, but he'd kept it from the rest of the family because he knew they'd worry about owing so much to the bank.

But now, with the money from the Indian Board of Cultural Affairs, Luca could pay off the loan and buy the new big top outright. 'When we come back to Castle Key next year,' Bella had told the friends, 'you won't recognize us. We'll be bigger and better than ever. Even without our ruby.'

'And finally,' Enzo Romaldi said as the applause died down, 'I have one last announcement. There are three very special people in the audience tonight.' He paused as Bella ran across the ring and whispered something in his ear. 'Sorry,' he said. 'My granddaughter has just corrected me. There are *four* very special people in the audience tonight.' He threw open his arms. 'Please would Jack, Scott, Emily and Drift join us in the ring.'

'What? *Us?*' Emily couldn't believe it.

Scott couldn't help blushing as the spotlight picked him out and he felt everyone staring. He raked his fingers through his hair and tried to look cool and laid-back about it all.

Jack had no such worries. He made his way along the row. 'Make way. Celebrity Guardian Angel coming through!'

Enzo shook them all by the hand.

Drift jumped down from Emily's arms, padded across the ring on bandaged paws and sat down next to Mimi.

Enzo spoke into the microphone. 'These brave and determined young people . . . and dog,' he added, smiling at Bella, 'have taught us that the true success of the Romaldi family circus lies in the talent and hard work of our performers and the support of our friends, not in the protection of a jewel. And, in recognition of their . . .'

' . . . *Quick thinking and decisive action!*' Scott, Jack, Emily and Bella chorused.

'Exactly!' Enzo laughed. 'We present you with these certificates, confirming that you are honorary members of the Romaldi family – and giving you free entry to the circus for life.'

'And if you fancy *joining* the circus,' Luca added with a grin, 'we're looking for some new recruits. We

174

need a couple more guys for the trapeze act and we're missing a contortionist too.'

Emily smiled and shook her head. After her experience in the Ali Baba jar she had no desire to be in a circus act again for a very long time.

'And Drift would be very welcome to work with Mimi as a double act,' Madame Zelda offered.

Drift and Mimi wagged their tails.

Jack thought for a moment. What could be more awesome than running away with the circus? But then he remembered the dawn rehearsals and the afternoon schoolwork and how hard it had been to catch the trapeze. And then there were those red sequined leotards!

Scott looked at Jack and Emily and laughed. Then he turned to Enzo. 'Thank you for the offer, Mr Romaldi, but I think we'll stick to *watching* the circus.'

'But we'll see you when we come back to Castle Key next summer,' Bella said. 'You *will* be here, won't you?'

Scott hugged his certificate to his chest. 'Of course we will!'

He couldn't think of anywhere else he'd rather be.

Don't miss the next exciting mystery
in the *Adventure Island* series

THE MYSTERY OF THE
VANISHING SKELETON

Available now!

Read on for a special preview
of the first chapter.

One

Return to Castle Key

J ack Carter leaped up to grab his backpack from the luggage rack. The journey from London to Cornwall had taken light years, but at last the train was pulling into Carrickstowe station. Jack felt as if he'd been stuck in one of those deep-freeze machines on a spaceship, voyaging to a distant galaxy. He poked his brother in the ribs. 'Come on, we're there!'

Scott – a year older at thirteen — considered himself

infinitely cooler and more laid-back than Jack. He raked his fingers through his floppy hair, stretched his legs and cracked his knuckles. 'Relax!' he sighed. 'Where's the fire?'

But Jack knew that beneath the oh-so-chilled exterior, Scott was just as excited as he was. It was funny, Jack thought. The first time they had come to Castle Key, at the beginning of the summer, they had both thought it was going to be the most boring holiday of their lives. Jack had actually spent the first night planning how to run away. How wrong could you be! As soon as the brothers had met Emily Wild – who lived in The Lighthouse at the end of the harbour – and her little dog Drift, it was as if they'd crossed over into another dimension: a dimension full of secret passages and haunted attics and buried treasure and cursed jewels. Yep, one way and another it had been quite a summer! So when Dad suggested Scott and Jack might like to go and stay with Aunt Kate again for the October half-term, while he attended an archaeology conference in Germany, they'd jumped at the chance.

They'd brought their bikes with them on the train and were soon cycling over the narrow causeway and heading south across the island. Jack gulped down the tang of the sea wafting over the heather and gorse and listened to the wailing of the seagulls overhead. His heart felt as if it were singing *We are the Champions* in a packed-out football stadium. Scott felt the same way too, going by the ear-to-ear grin on his face as he sped along.

It was great to be back!

They crossed the common, free-wheeled into the village and raced along the high street. At last they turned into Church Lane and stood up on the pedals to climb the steep hill. They threw their bikes against the garden wall and ran up the path.

Aunt Kate was waiting for them in the doorway of Stone Cottage, smiling and patting down flyaway wisps of white hair. 'Ah, there you are,' she said, as if they'd just popped out for a quick bike ride. 'I've made some nice gingerbread for you.'

Jack grinned. Aunt Kate's cooking was another reason he'd been looking forward to coming back to Castle Key.

The brothers hugged their great-aunt, but they hadn't even got past the doorstep when they heard someone calling their names. They turned to see Emily cycling up the lane, her long brown hair flying and her trusty bag slung over her shoulder – no doubt stuffed full of crime-busting gadgets and evidence-collecting kit. Drift was in the basket on the back, of course, his tongue hanging out and his ears streaming back. *Emily without Drift would be like chips without ketchup,* Jack thought.

Like hot chocolate without marshmallows. Some things were just meant to be together. 'Wow! She got here fast,' he said.

'This *is* Emily we're talking about,' Scott reminded him. 'She'll have been scanning the road with her binoculars for hours.'

Emily screeched to a halt and ran to hug Scott and Jack. She hesitated, suddenly a little shy. Maybe hugs would be too soppy? She held up her hands for high-fives instead. Drift had no such qualms. He threw himself into Jack's arms and gave his nose a big slobbery lick. Then he launched himself at Scott to give him the same welcome.

'Yeah, it's great to see you too, Drifty!' Jack laughed. 'I can't tell you how much I've missed having a faceful of dog drool!'

'Hey, Em!' Scott said. 'Have you got a fantastic new investigation lined up for us yet?'

'Well, I don't know whether this counts as *fantastic*,' Emily replied, following the boys as they lugged their backpacks into the cottage. 'Or even as an investigation really, but Vicky White just called me from Roshendra Farm. Someone has let all the rabbits out of their hutches.'

Jack gripped his throat and staggered backwards across the living room. 'Oh, no!' he gurgled. 'Blood-crazed rabbits rampaging across the island, slaughtering the livestock, terrorising the tourists . . .'

182

'I'll call in the army,' Scott said. 'You alert the Prime Minister, Em. He'll probably want to declare a state of national emergency.'

Emily rolled her eyes. She'd forgotten how maddening the boys could be when they got started. 'They're not *ordinary* rabbits,' she began to explain.

Scott bugged his eyes at Jack. 'It's even worse than we thought. *Mutant bunnies!*'

Emily laughed. 'They're Mrs White's *prize-winning* rabbits. They're really valuable. Vicky asked if we'd go and help round them up.'

Jack looked at Aunt Kate. *Would it be rude to rush off so soon?* he wondered. And there *was* that plate of gingerbread on the table.

'Go on!' Aunt Kate laughed. 'You can unpack when you get back. And I'll put the gingerbread in a bag for you to take with you.'

—

The friends found Vicky White crawling around the farmyard. 'I came home from university for a quiet weekend,' she said from behind an old pigsty. There were twigs in her long blonde plaits and mud all over her jeans. 'Not much chance of that! Mum's just had an operation on her leg and Dad's off at a cattle market, so I've been trying to round up these little terrors on my own.' She stood up, cradling a ball of white fluff in her arms.

'Is that a *rabbit*?' Jack asked. 'It looks more like a giant powder puff.'

'He's an angora,' Vicky explained. 'Meet *Roshendra Majestic Snowball*. He won Best in Show last year.'

Emily stroked the rabbit's silky fur.

Vicky settled Snowball back into his hutch in the barn. Then she sighed. 'There are still about twenty more on the loose.'

'So what are we waiting for?' Jack asked. 'Let's get bunny-wrangling!'

—

An hour later all but one of the rabbits were accounted for. It was only half past six but the light was fading fast and a thick fog was settling across the fields. The long warm evenings of summer seemed a distant memory.

Suddenly Jack glimpsed a shadowy form scampering into the undergrowth. 'Gotcha!' he cried, diving into a ditch.

'Woof!'

Woof? Since when did rabbits bark? Jack sat up with a handful of black and tan fur. 'Oh, Drift, it's you!'

Drift pounced on Jack, wagging his tail in bliss. Whoever invented this Find the Rabbit game was a genius in Drift's book. Of course, it would be even better if he could *chase* the rabbits too, but Emily had told him they were Special Rabbits and chasing was strictly off-limits. And now there was wrestling with Jack. It was heaven in a dog-bowl. *There goes another rabbit!* Drift darted through the hedge and gave the signal.

'Drift's barking. Look, he's found the missing rabbit!' Emily scooped a bundle of grey fluff out of the grass and handed it to Vicky.

Vicky returned the rabbit to its hutch, checked all the doors and locked the barn. 'Thanks for coming to the rescue,' she said. 'I don't know where I'd be without you guys.'

Prison, probably, Scott thought. During their first adventure in Castle Key, Vicky White had been framed for the theft of Saxon treasure from the castle museum – until Scott, Jack and Emily discovered the identity of the real culprit and proved her innocence.

Mrs White appeared at the door of the farmhouse, hobbling with a walking stick. The news that her beloved bunnies were safely back in their hutches brought tears to her eyes. She insisted that the friends come in and sit down at the enormous kitchen table, which she rapidly loaded with cakes and hot chocolate. Drift munched on a biscuit, then curled up next to a jowly old Labrador in front of the old-fashioned fireplace.

Vicky frowned into her mug. 'I just can't understand why anyone would go round letting rabbits out in the first place.'

'Are you *sure* it was deliberate?' Emily asked.

Vicky nodded. 'I know I locked up properly after I

fed them at lunchtime. When Mum went to check them this afternoon, all the hutches and the barn door were open. Rabbits are smarter than you'd think but they haven't learned how to open padlocks yet.'

The kitchen door swung open and Laura Roberts padded in in her socks, having pulled off her muddy riding boots in the porch. With her blonde ponytail and blue eyes, Laura could have been mistaken for Vicky's younger sister, but she worked in the stables attached to the farm. She was happy to see the friends and joined them at the table. Conversation soon turned back to the puzzle of the escaping rabbits.

'Have you seen anyone suspicious hanging around the farm today?' Vicky asked Laura.

Laura shrugged. 'No, not really.'

Emily's ears pricked up. *Not really* sounded a lot like yes. 'You *did* see someone, then? When was this?'

'I was out leading a ride this afternoon. I thought I saw something flitting through the trees at the edge of the moor.'

'What kind of something?' Scott probed.

'I know this sounds crazy but I thought it was a skeleton for a moment.' Laura laughed and blew onto her hot chocolate. 'I turned to see if any of the kids on the ride had seen it but when I looked back it'd gone.' She paused and shuddered. 'It really gave me the creeps, actually. But it was probably just branches blowing in the wind. It *was* getting quite foggy.'

'You've been watching too many horror films,' Vicky laughed.

Jack looked at Scott and Emily. *Padlocks opening by themselves?* he wondered. *Skeletons prowling the misty moors?*

Only in Castle Key could a few escaped rabbits sound like the start of a whole new mystery!

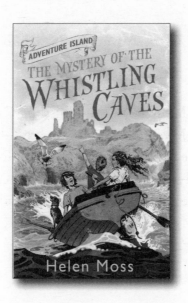

Emily and Drift take Scott and Jack to see the
amazing Whistling Caves – but the caves are
strangely silent! Legend has it this means the castle
will be attacked, and when priceless treasures are
stolen from the castle museum it seems the legend
is true! But how did the thief escape, and why did
the caves stop whistling?

Join Scott, Jack, Emily and Drift as they try to
solve the mystery and find the stolen treasure!

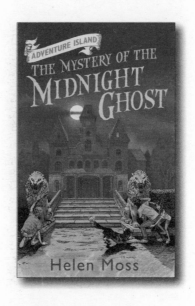

ADVENTURE ISLAND

THE MYSTERY OF THE MIDNIGHT GHOST

Helen Moss

Lights. Camera. Action!

An Agent Diamond movie is being filmed at creepy Pendragon Manor, but when the star of the film suddenly vanishes, Scott, Jack, Emily and Drift realize they have a new mystery to solve.

Follow the friends on this spooky adventure as they try to uncover the secret of the Midnight Ghost!

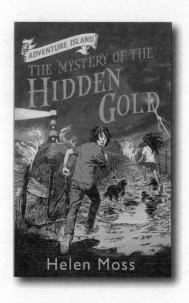

ADVENTURE ISLAND

THE MYSTERY OF THE HIDDEN GOLD

Helen Moss

A game of hide and seek in The Lighthouse during a violent thunder storm leads to an amazing discovery – a tattered old treasure map! Scott, Jack and Emily can't wait to search for the hidden gold but first they must solve the clues to uncover its secret hiding place. And someone else is after the gold too – someone who doesn't plan to let anyone get in their way!

Can the friends figure out the map, outwit their enemy and find the hidden treasure?

When thieves raid the house of a neighbour,
Emily, Jack and Scott are ready to investigate. But,
strangely, the neighbour doesn't seem to want the
thieves to be caught!

The burglars didn't escape with much this time but
could the raid be connected to a much older crime
involving millions of pounds? The friends begin to
uncover the truth, but are they leading themselves
into serious danger?